T·H·E
NAKED BEAR

Folktales of the Iroquois

Edited by *John Bierhorst*

Illustrated by *Dirk Zimmer*

WILLIAM MORROW AND COMPANY

New York

Library of Congress Cataloging-in-Publication Data
Bierhorst, John/The naked bear

Summary/A collection of sixteen traditional tales
told by the Iroquois Indians, some featuring talking
animals and some presenting terrifying flesh-eating creatures
such as the Naked Bear, the Stone Coat, and the Whirlwinds.
1. Iroquois Indians—Legends. 2. Indians of North America—Legends.
[1. Iroquois Indians—Legends. 2. Indians of North America—Legends]
I. Bierhorst, John. II. Zimmer, Dirk, ill.
E99.17N35 1987   398.2'08997   86-21836
ISBN 0-688-06422-1

Contents

Until a thousand years ago the people who lived in the region now known as New York State were wanderers, hunting birds and animals and gathering wild plants. With the discovery of a kind of corn that could be grown in the cold climate west of the Catskills and near the shores of Lake Ontario, the people settled in villages and began to keep gardens. Over the centuries these villagers gradually acquired the customs, the form of government, the ceremonies—and the stories—that have come to be known as Iroquoian.

Iroquois traditions, including folktales, are therefore many hundreds of years old. Although we cannot be completely sure what Iroquois stories sounded like in the days before the first Europeans arrived, we can assume that they were not too different from the versions that were finally written down in the 1880s and that form the basis for this book. These are the tales of boy heroes, cannibals, stone giants, monster bears, and the trickster Turtle that are considered typical of the New York Indians.

The Iroquois who were still telling the old stories in the late nineteenth century were people who lived in ordinary-looking carpenter-built houses in small towns and rural settlements in the western part of the state. The women, some of them, wore long calico dresses, and the men, like other American men of that time, wore shirts with cuffs and collars and trousers with suspenders buttoned to the waistband. Children in miniature versions of the same attire joined the circle as family and friends took their places on wooden chairs or benches in front of a fireplace or an iron stove.

But in the stories themselves a different world came to life.

"There was a bark lodge," the storyteller would begin, and at once the listeners would be taken back to the days when their ancestors had lived in longhouses framed with arched saplings covered in elm bark, with a bark-flap door at either end. "In those ancient times," as the storytellers were fond of saying, the rafters would be hung with dried meat, and people in buckskin and fur robes would be sitting on mats or lounging on platform beds. Bear oil or spicebush tea might be served, and the fire in the open pit, with its smoke hole overhead, would be burning strips of bark from a shagbark hickory.

Yet, despite obvious differences, Iroquois storytelling sessions of the 1880s had much in common with those of the long-gone past. Professional storytellers still went from house to house and expected to be paid with small gifts of food, tobacco, or other items. In a manner of speaking, at least, the storyteller, as in the old days, would still arrive with his "bag," formerly an actual pouch filled with trinkets that represented the different tales he knew. When it was time for the performance to begin, he might say, "Now I will tell you a story," to which the listeners would reply, "Heh!"

As the tale progressed, the audience was supposed to interrupt with occasional sounds of approval. If the responses died away, the storyteller would stop and ask what was the matter, and if someone fell asleep, he would "tie off the bag," and no amount of pleading could persuade him to reopen it.

Times have changed for the Iroquois, no less than for American society as a whole. Improved transportation, the use of radio, and, finally, the coming of television have weakened the demand for the kind of entertainment old-time storytellers could provide. By the 1930s the professional storyteller was no longer a fixture in Iroquois communities. In the 1980s, interestingly, there were still people who remembered some of the old tales. But these stories, if told at all, were told in a deliberate effort to revive the past or were written down with the help of university-trained linguists in order to preserve what remained of the native language.

The Five Nations

The telling of folktales requires expert language skills and takes for granted a group of listeners that can appreciate half-hidden jokes, double meanings, and all the little oddities of expression that give a story its life. At the same time, both the teller and the audience, for all their expertise, must be willing to give themselves over to the spell of enchantment.

For the Iroquois today, such conditions are hard to meet. It would be wrong to think, however, that Iroquois language arts are about to die out.

Elaborate speeches used in religious and political ceremonies, as well as songs, continue to be very much alive. These forms of expression are easier to keep up than storytelling. Yet their value is considerable. The ability to pass the language from one generation to the next, even if only for ritual use, is one of the important ways in which the Five Nations of the Iroquois—Mohawk, Oneida, Onondaga, Cayuga, and Seneca—command the respect of the outside world.

Of these five original nations, all but the Cayuga continue to hold tribal lands in New York State, and in the mid-1980s the Cayuga claim to portions of Seneca and Cayuga counties, thirty miles west of Syracuse, was being considered by the United States Congress. A sixth nation, the Tuscarora, formerly of North Carolina but now adopted by the New York Iroquois, have lands in Erie County just north of Niagara Falls.

Tuscarora, although an Iroquoian language, is somewhat different from the languages of the old Five Nations, almost as different as French and Spanish. Within the Five Nations the languages are very close, closer than Spanish and Portuguese. Today all six languages are spoken in New York, and in parts of southern Canada as well, especially on the Six Nations Reserve in Ontario, where many Iroquois moved after the American Revolution.

Compared to other Indian groups, the Five Nations are well known to the outside world. With the exception of the Navajo and the Eskimo, more has been written about them than about any other native people north of Mexico.

Because they controlled the trade route between the Great Lakes and the Hudson Valley and because, moreover, they acted jointly as a league, the Iroquois during colonial times enjoyed a position of enviable power. Had they sided with the French instead of the English in the French and Indian War, the map of North America might be different today.

In the opinion of Lewis Henry Morgan, the most important of the early writers on the Iroquois, the Five Nations exerted greater political influence than any other American Indian group except for the Aztecs and the Incas. Morgan no doubt was recalling that Iroquois war parties once roamed over a territory stretching from Montreal to present-day Chicago and as far south as the Carolinas. Arthur Parker, the eminent Iroquois specialist, who wrote during the first few decades of this century, believed that the Iroquois was the "Indian of Indians," and applying the same generalization in a narrower sphere, he declared that Iroquois folktales were the "classics" of all the unwritten literature of native America.

Enthusiasm for the Iroquois can be said to have had its start in the 1600s, when French missionaries began writing colorful reports on the Huron Indians of southern Ontario. Although distinct from the Five Nations, the Huron were an Iroquoian people, whose customs—including folktales—were similar to those of the Iroquois proper.

By 1750 interest in the native peoples of the New World had declined, though the Iroquois are mentioned briefly in a great many reports, journals, and histories of the period. Thomas Jefferson admired the Iroquois League, and George Washington as a young man wrote an account of an Iroquois dance. Information in depth did not become available, however, until Morgan's *League of the Iroquois,* published in 1851. Morgan, and later writers as well, concentrated on the Seneca, the westernmost of the Five Nations, the one with the largest population and the best-preserved traditions.

The result is that much of what we know today about Five Nations religion, art, music, and especially folktales comes from the Seneca. In fact, the great folktale collections were made in a single Seneca community, the Cattaraugus Reservation, thirty miles south of the city of Buffalo.

All the tales in this book derive ultimately from Cattaraugus sources. And yet, if these are compared with other, lesser collections, notably from the Onondaga and the Cayuga, it can be safely said that the Seneca stories are representative of the folk literature of the Five Nations as a whole.

The Naked Bear

Whether Iroquois folktales are the "classics" of American Indian lore, as Parker imagined, it is certainly true that in no other body of Indian tales are there so many happy endings or such a modern sense of evil punished and virtue rewarded. The reason, perhaps, is that the Iroquois have been carefully absorbing European influences for more than three hundred years.

Nevertheless, the plots and even the minor incidents are thoroughly grounded in Indian tradition. In fact, many of the stories, such as Two Feathers, Animal-Foot Hitter, and Turtle's War Party, are variants of tales told by Plains and Great Lakes tribes. To this shared material the Iroquois have added touches of local color and a cast of supernatural characters that, if not uniquely Iroquoian, reach their fullest development in Iroquois lore. Included in this group are the Whirlwinds, also called Flying Heads, the Stone Coats, the Great Defender, and the Naked Bear. Among old-time Iroquois listeners these figures needed no introduction.

Everyone knew, for example, that the Naked Bear had smooth, hairless skin. Actually, it was not completely naked but had a narrow ridge of hair down its backbone or, sometimes, just a tuft at the end of its tail. Some said it was so huge that its back could be seen above the treetops when it walked through the woods.

All sources agree that the Naked Bear could not be killed by ordinary means. Since its ribs were grown together in a solid wall, no arrow could penetrate its chest cavity. Even so, the monster's heart was not in its chest but in one of its paws. Therefore the knowledgeable hero waited patiently for the creature to lift its paw, revealing a small patch of white (some said black), then aimed his arrow at this vital spot.

The Naked Bear's most significant, most basic trait is one that it shares with the only slightly less terrifying Stone Coat. To use the polite word familiar to readers of European fairy tales, the Naked Bear is an ogre. However, translators of Iroquois lore have always stated the matter more bluntly, writing either "man-eater" or "cannibal."

Man-eaters of whatever kind are the hallmark of Five Nations folklore. They crop up everywhere, at home and in the woods, sniffing out human flesh, chasing children to the ends of the earth, and luring unwary travelers into their cooking pots. Occasionally they can be reformed, but it is usually necessary to put them to death.

In the case of the Stone Coat, the task is made easier by the creature's dim-wittedness and by the very fact of its hard, stiff covering, which prevents it from turning its head to look around. Also, it is easily drowned, if it can be maneuvered to the edge of deep water, because, being so heavy, it cannot swim.

According to one account, Stone Coats originated when a giant's children rubbed themselves with sand until their skin became "hard and calloused like a woman's hand when the harvest is over." It follows that arrows do not hurt Stone Coats. But they can sometimes be killed by a club made of basswood, which, like red willow, has magic properties.

Though dangerous, Stone Coats can be helpful if they are approached in a friendly manner. For instance, it is said that a young Seneca once acquired hunting luck by marrying the daughter of the chief of the Stone Coats.

More likely to be helpful are the horrific Whirlwinds, who typically appear as disembodied heads with long hair and fiery eyes. When not eating human flesh, they sweep through the forest, devouring rocks and sticks. Nevertheless, it is sometimes possible to bring one home, and if it is given a nest to live in and plenty of sticks to eat, it will help out by keeping witches away.

More helpful yet is the Great Wind, or Great Defender, who blows away disease and often appears unexpectedly in folktales, giving the hero a piece of advice or pointing him in the right direction.

Any of these supernaturals, incidentally, can live as an ordinary human being. In one story we meet a nice Whirlwind family, whose children do not even realize they are Whirlwinds until they learn the truth from their grandmother. In another story a strange boy wins respect by killing the Naked Bear. After a while people begin to realize that the boy is actually a Stone Coat, "though he does not look like one."

The same is true of ordinary animals, such as moose, swans, partridges, or turtles. In the stories they may act and look like humans. But if they do, it is understood that these are tales of the distant past and such things would not be possible today.

The idea of a remote time when animals were people is an important feature of many Indian mythologies, especially those in which the hero is a trickster like Coyote, Hare, or Raven. But Iroquois mythology, as distinguished from folklore, does not involve animal people or a trickster hero. On the contrary, the sacred story of the Five Nations tells of a woman who descended from the sky and became the grandmother of twin boys who shaped the world. Enriched with numerous episodes stretched out over several generations, this epic may be compared to the Bible of Christianity.

Possibly the Iroquois folktales, with their hints of monster people and animal people, hark back to a much older body of myth that was replaced by the sacred epic. In any case, it should be made clear that the folktales in this book do not represent the mythology, or sacred lore, of the Iroquois. Although, like all folktales, they had educational value for young people, reinforcing behavior patterns and long-standing customs, they were told primarily for entertainment.

The Sources

The single most important collection of Iroquois stories is the one made by the folklorist Jeremiah Curtin, known also for his studies of Russian, Irish, and California Indian lore, carried out during the second half of the nineteenth century. His Iroquois work began when he was hired by the Smithsonian Institution in 1883. During that year, after studying Seneca for a few months with a native speaker who had been brought to the Smithsonian's offices in Washington, Curtin traveled to the Cattaraugus Reservation, where he gathered some 130 stories. Evidently he returned to Cattaraugus once or twice before ending his service with the Smithsonian in 1891, but most of his Seneca tales seem to have been collected that first year.

An additional thirty or more stories were collected in 1896, also at Cattaraugus, by J. N. B. Hewitt, an Iroquois specialist and permanent staff member of the Smithsonian. Hewitt's manuscripts, as Curtin's had been, were deposited at the Smithsonian, where they may still be consulted. However, in 1918, after Curtin's death, Hewitt published 106 of Curtin's stories, together with twenty-nine of his own, all carefully revised, in a massive report entitled "Seneca Fiction."

In 1903, again at Cattaraugus, Arthur Parker made a new collection of stories, which he later published in his *Seneca Myths and Folk Tales*. Although of great value, Parker's versions were not as carefully prepared as Curtin's and Hewitt's had been. In general they are shorter and translated with greater freedom. Other noteworthy collections of the period, including those made by Erminnie Smith, apparently at Cattaraugus and other locations, and F. W. Waugh, mostly at Six Nations, are also available.

If the reputation of Iroquois folktales can be said to rest on Curtin's and Hewitt's "Seneca Fiction," it is not only because theirs is the largest collection but because it most convincingly preserves the flavor of old-time Iroquois speech. Nevertheless, questions arise.

In a recent conversation with a Seneca traditionalist from the Six Nations Reserve, I asked if any of the old stories were being kept up and received the information that they were. But when I asked about Iroquois stories in English, I was told, "There's a problem here. The trouble is, they don't sound right in English. You have to use too many words."

This observation, true of any translation from Seneca into a European language, applies especially well to the versions made by Hewitt. Wordiness is both the virtue and the shortcoming of his style—a virtue because shades of meaning are preserved. But the trade-off is that the pace of the story becomes unbearably slow.

Curtin's versions move a little more briskly. However, they lack richness and perhaps accuracy. In the story Mother Swan's Daughters, Curtin wrote the sentence "If we can get our basket we will go home," which Hewitt corrected to "If we could get the basket, we might go on." This is confirmed by a variant that reads: "They . . . started on with their basket." Without Hewitt's seemingly minor repair, the whole passage is confusing.

But in the same story Hewitt has the mother complaining about having to eat "moss," where Curtin had written "mushrooms." The Seneca word is *onehsa,* which modern speakers define as "fungus," suggesting that Curtin may have been correct after all.

Far from rare, such discrepancies abound in the Curtin stories that Hewitt revised. More puzzling still are the sentences and often whole paragraphs that mysteriously appear, or drop out, in one translation or the other. Possibly a careful examination of the Seneca manuscripts could resolve some of these problems. Moreover, it could bring to light the stories that Hewitt suppressed. So enormous a project has not been undertaken, or even considered, in the preparation of this book, which is intended only as a step toward making Iroquois folktales better known.

The versions given here were drawn primarily from the Curtin and Hewitt translations, after making a set of lists that bring together, for comparison, all the variants of particular story types, characters, and minor incidents. The lists were then expanded to include the collections made by Parker and others, resulting in what might be called a concordance to Five Nations folklore.

With this in hand it was possible to identify the storytellers' favorites, command a full view of the variants, and select the strongest, clearest wordings in each case. Parker, in his *Seneca Myths and Folk Tales,* had used the same kind of approach, combining two or more variants to produce a single reading of a particular tale. The more massive discrepancies between Curtin's and Hewitt's readings suggest that they, too, may have used this method to some extent.

The advantage here is that a modest-sized book can be made to hold a representative selection of Iroquois folktales—abridged and recombined, but not retold. In other words, every figure of speech, like every detail of plot, has its source in the native texts. In addition, it should be emphasized that the term "folktales," as here defined, means stories of romance or adventure, strictly speaking. More accessible than sacred lore, which requires careful study, yet more substantial than the anecdotes and folkloric hear-say that often pass as folktales, these are the shapely, richly detailed stories that can slip across cultural boundaries and travel around the world. It is hoped the present collection will help bring them to the wider audience that they deserve.

J.B.

West Shokan, N.Y.
January 1986

THE NAKED BEAR
FOLKTALES OF THE IROQUOIS

Chestnut Pudding

In a small lodge deep in the woods an old woman lived with her grandson. Every day she would cook food for the little boy, but she herself would never eat.

One evening, when the fire was hot and potatoes and moss were simmering, the boy asked his grandmother to sit down and have supper with him. "I will eat some other time," she said. "This food is for you alone."

The boy finished, then said, "Oh, grandmother, I am sleepy. I have to lie down now and get some rest," and with these words he wrapped himself in an old piece of skin and began to snore as if he were sound asleep.

But the skin had a tiny hole in it, and through the hole the boy was watching to see what his grandmother would do.

When the old woman was satisfied that her grandson was sleeping, she took out a bark case from under her bed and carefully opened it. Inside were a tiny kettle, a red-willow wand, and a piece of food. Holding the food in her hand, she scraped off a few crumbs into the kettle and added water.

When it began to boil, she tapped the kettle gently with the wand and sang the words, "Now, my kettle, I want you to grow." As she sang, the kettle became large and filled up with pudding.

She ate the pudding quickly, and as soon as she was finished, she washed the kettle, shook it to make it small again, then put everything back in the hiding place under her bed.

The next day, while the grandmother was out getting firewood, the boy searched under her bed until he found the things he had seen her use the night before. The tiny piece of food seemed hardly enough for one portion, so he scraped all of it into the kettle and began to tap with the wand.

The kettle became enormous. It grew so large the boy had to use a paddle to stir the pudding. As it boiled, making the sound bub bub bub bub bub, it began to overflow and fill the room around the fire.

The boy jumped onto the bed and kept stirring. Then he climbed to the rafters and finally to the roof. Running around the smoke hole, he kept on stirring the pudding, which now filled the entire lodge.

Suddenly he saw his grandmother hurrying out of the woods. Looking up, she could see her grandson running in circles on the roof. When she reached the door of the lodge, she saw the bark flaps bulging and the pudding already starting to spill out.

Immediately she blew on the pudding, and it shrank back. She blew harder. It shrank more, and she kept on blowing until it was all gone. Then she called to her grandson, "Come, now, get down from there."

Her voice was sad. As the boy crawled off the roof, she said to him, "You have used up all my food. There is nothing else I can eat. That little piece would have lasted me many years."

Wrapping herself in a skin robe, she added, "I may as well lie down right here. Hunger will finish me off." Having said this, she lay on the ground and covered herself up completely.

"Grandmother," cried the boy, "what is the name of this food?"

"It is called chestnut," she said, speaking through the robe.

"And where does it grow?"

"It is of no use for me to tell you. How could you ever get to it? You are only a little boy." Her voice was muffled. But she continued, saying, "The chestnut tree is owned by seven sisters, who are witches, and the path to their lodge is guarded by living things that would attack you."

"And where is the path?"

"Toward the rising sun."

Then the boy left on a swift run. All day he raced, until the sun was low in the west and he saw as he passed through a clearing that the woods' edges were hidden in dew clouds. There he built a fire and camped for the night.

Standing close to the fire and holding a pinch of tobacco he had taken from his pouch, he said, "Come, now, listen to me, you, all kinds of animals and you, too, who have formed and made my life." With these words he threw the tobacco into the fire, then cried out, "Now, listen. The smoke is rising. I ask you to help me."

The next morning he started early, hurrying on toward the east. It wasn't long before he came to a steep gorge, too steep to climb into and too wide to jump across. Then he talked to the gorge: "Earth, why are you broken? This is unheard of. I won't allow it. Close up!" And the earth closed with a loud snap.

He kept on until he came to two giant rattlesnakes standing guard over the path. They opened their jaws and began to rattle. But the boy talked to them: "Rattlesnakes, go away. Get out of my path. Be ashamed!"

Frightened, the rattlesnakes closed their jaws and hurried off into the woods.

The boy ran on. Suddenly two panthers appeared, one on each side of the path. He ran straight toward them. "Panthers," he said, "you are free to go. Get out of my way!"

Surprised by the boy's words, the panthers drew back and let him pass.

He ran on, until at last the trees began to thin out and he could see a lodge in the distance at the far side of a clearing. Next to the lodge stood the chestnut tree, guarded by an eagle perched at the top.

Knowing that he would have to be careful, the boy called for a mole, saying, "Now, my friend, I want you to come to me. Come to me, you mole." In a short time the leaves began to rustle at his feet, and a mole appeared, asking, "What do you want?"

The boy replied, "My grandmother is in trouble. I scraped away her last chestnut. Now you must help me get her some more. Let me fit inside your body. Take me underground to that tree in the far corner of the clearing, and don't let the eagle hear us."

When the boy had entered the mole's body, it made its way quickly to the roots of the tree. Then it pushed its nose and mouth up through the dry leaves, and the boy stuck his ear out of the mole's mouth to listen for sounds from the lodge.

Hearing nothing, he jumped to his full size, shook a

bag from his pouch, and filled it with chestnuts. He had turned to go and was just running off when the eagle heard him and gave a scream.

At once the seven sisters came out of their lodge, waving their war clubs, shouting, "Someone has stolen our chestnuts. Catch him!"

The boy ran as fast as he could, but the witches kept coming nearer. He could hear their footsteps close behind him. Suddenly he turned around and began to beat on the bag of chestnuts as though it were a drum. "Now you will dance," he cried. And he sang:

to the upper side

of the sky

to the upper side

of the sky

and never return

and never return

He kept on drumming as the sisters rose into the air, half as high as the tallest trees, and all the while they were dancing. They rose still higher and soon disappeared in the sky.

The boy ran on, not stopping until the sun went under the hills and the black night came. Again he made camp, and in the morning he continued on his way, arriving at his grandmother's in time to hear her say, "Oh, grandson, you have come, and I am still alive." The boy rushed into the lodge, letting the bag of chestnuts fall—with the sound pumh! It was very heavy.

"Grandson, tell me," cried the old woman, "how did you ever do it?"

"I, of course, know how I did it, but I will tell you only this: that I got rid of all those witches."

"So be it," she said. "What a wonderful thing this is." Then they scattered handfuls of chestnuts, and many were planted.

From that time on, the grandmother always had enough to eat, and somewhere, deep in the woods, they say, she is still making chestnut puddings.

Two Feathers

In times past, a shaman was living in a bark lodge with his nephew, Listener, a boy just growing up. The uncle was named Two Feathers. One day the uncle said to the boy, "You have grown to manhood and must marry a wife. Come now! I will clean you up for the occasion."

Nearby hung a bear's bladder filled with sunflower oil. The uncle took some in his hand and rubbed it all over the boy's body. "That's fine," he said. "Now stand facing me. Let me look at you, because I don't know how handsome you are."

The uncle eyed him carefully. "Come here," he said. "I am not satisfied."

Again he poured sunflower oil into the palm of his hand, and this time he rubbed the boy's face. "Now stand back again."

The boy stood back. "Ah," said the uncle, "there is nowhere living another young man as handsome. Now come to me. This is what you shall be named: Two Feathers you shall be called, and in all the distant places where people dwell the sound has gone, saying of you,

'He is a great hunter of all kinds of animals.' Your name is one which is obeyed and which is heard in distant places of the land."

Then the old shaman brought out a robe of raccoon skins and looked at it carefully. The fur was long and glossy. "No," he said, "this is not fine enough."

Again reaching into his bark chest of treasures, he took out a wildcat robe. There were ears sewed around the neck, and eyes on the sleeves. "All right, this will do." But his heart changed, and he said, "No, it is not excellent."

Once more he reached into the chest. This time he took out a panther skin with the head of the animal formed into a cap. When the wearer of this wonderful robe became excited, the head would cry out in anger. In the cap the uncle placed two loon feathers, which sang at all times. "Now people will see you as you are," he said.

To complete the outfit, he handed his nephew a fisher-skin pouch and told him to sit down. The boy did so, and opening the pouch, he took out a pipe and filled it with red-willow bark. Immediately two spirit girls and two trick pigeons leaped out of the pouch. The girls brought the fire to light his pipe, and as soon as the pipe was put to his mouth, the pigeons, which were perched on the stem, rustled their wings and cooed. When the young man exhaled, wampum beads fell out of his mouth and rattled on the ground.

"Now that you are ready," said the uncle, "you must travel east. Keep going until you come to a valley, and there you will find a village, also the lodge of a great witch woman who is seeking a husband for her daughter. Near her lodge grows a tall hickory tree with an eagle on top. Whoever can bring down the eagle will get the daughter. People go there from every direction to shoot at it, but no one has hit it yet. On the trail you must keep no man company. Sleep alone, and hurry."

The young nephew set out at once, and finding the trail, he traveled along until the sun was sinking low and its red rays shot upward through the treetops.

When he had made camp and had taken off his fine clothes, laying them under a covering of hemlock branches, an old man came to his fire and said, "Let me sit across from you. I am on my way to the village nearby, but it is too late to go farther now. We will go together in the morning. To pass the time I will tell you stories."

Without thinking, the young man agreed. Then the stranger began telling his stories, and the boy responded, "Heh!" But after a while, as the boy grew sleepy, the responses stopped.

Quietly the old man got up and put on the boy's clothes, leaving his own ragged garments in their place. In the morning when the young man awoke, he found himself alone and saw that his good clothes had been stolen. Ashamed, he put on the garments left by the stranger and continued his journey to the old woman's lodge.

He had not gone far when he heard sounds in the distance, telling him he had arrived at the place where people were shooting. Looking up, he could see the eagle on the great hickory tree rising above the forest.

Sometimes an arrow would come close to the eagle, and it would flap its wings. At this the crowd would give a loud shout of encouragement, and the old woman would run out of her lodge, saying, "Who is it that has become my son-in-law?" But the people would answer, "It is not true that someone has hit it."

Unnoticed, the young man aimed an arrow, and without a hitch it flew into the center of the bird's body, causing it to fall over with wings feebly flapping. The crowd cheered—so loudly you would think the sound had hit the sky.

But a stranger wearing a panther-skin robe pushed through the crowd and snatched the eagle before the young man could reach it. Seeing his fine clothes, the old woman said, "At last our man is coming to us."

The daughter protested, insisting that this was not the right person. But her mother said, "My promise must be kept," and she announced the marriage.

Taking the stranger by the arm, the old woman led him into her lodge, asking, "What can you do for me?" The man opened his fisher-skin pouch, and the fisher bit his finger. Then out came the two spirit girls, but when he told them to bring an ember to light his pipe, they did not move.

"My little girls are shy in front of all these people," he said. Taking a hot coal from the fire, he lit the pipe himself. But as he smoked, no wampum fell from his mouth, and the pigeons perched on the pipestem seemed almost dead. Their heads were hanging limp.

The mother-in-law, already angry, turned away in disgust. That evening the young woman would not go near the man who was said to be her husband but, rolling herself up in a bearskin, slept apart.

As soon as the lodge was quiet, Two Feathers came inside and took back the panther robe and the fisher-skin pouch that had been stolen from him the night before. In the morning, when he put them on, the cap, which had been silent, began to roar, and the loon feathers were singing.

When he came to greet the old woman, her daughter rushed forward joyfully, saying, "That is the man! That is the man!"

All right, but where was the one who had been called her husband? They found him still in bed, all doubled up and coughing horribly. Since the arrow that had killed the eagle was unlike his arrows but just like the ones in Two Feathers' quiver, the people were convinced that the old man was a deceiver, and they threw him out of the lodge.

The mother announced to all the people, "My daughter is now married." Then she spread a deerskin in front of her son-in-law and said, "What can you do for me?"

As he opened his pouch, the two girls jumped out of it, followed by the two pigeons. The girls, running nimbly to the fire, brought coals for lighting the pipe. The pigeons hopped up onto the pipestem and rustled their wings and cooed.

As the pipe burned, it gave off the good-smelling odor of hemlock gum, spicebush, and red-willow bark. Then the young man drew in the smoke with the sound hukt!, and when he exhaled, saying, "Hwuw!" the wampum beads fell out of his mouth with the sound da!

The mother-in-law picked up a large quantity of beads from the deerskin. Some of the beads rolled off, and all

the people scrambled for them. In the confusion they made a great uproar, as each one tried to get as many as he possibly could. When it was over, the people, well satisfied, returned to their homes.

After this the couple lived quietly together for a long time.

One day Two Feathers said to his mother-in-law, "I am thinking that my wife and I will return to my uncle's lodge. Now, my mother-in-law, I will tell you what I am thinking. I am not certain that you would be willing for me to suggest that you and my old uncle should care for each other. You two are fine-looking and about the same in age and bodily condition. But how is it? Would you agree?"

"Oh, my son!" said the mother-in-law. "Your thought suits me. What you have said will happen, provided your uncle is still in good health."

Then they departed on their long journey, making camp at night. When they reached the uncle's lodge, they found him dressed and ready to greet them. As they entered, the old man, tapping his bench, said to the mother-in-law, "Here you may sit."

She took her seat beside him, and the nephew and his wife sat on the opposite side of the fire. Then the uncle said to his nephew, "I am thankful that you have come. Now you must hunt, and mother and daughter will live well."

So Two Feathers spent his time hunting. Day after day he hunted. He knew exactly what animals to kill. And so it happened in the ancient time that they lived together in great contentment.

This is the end of the tale.

The Whirlwinds and the Stone Coats

An old Whirlwind woman, the oldest of her people, lived in the woods with two grandchildren, a boy and a girl.

One day while the old woman was out, a female Stone Coat came into the lodge and with one huge hand picked up the little girl. After speaking kindly to her, saying that she was a good little thing, she swallowed her.

Then she began to talk to the boy, telling him how beautiful he was, but, thinking she would save him for later, she did not eat him. Sitting down on the bed, she said, "Climb on my back, and I will take you to find your grandmother."

Terrified, the boy climbed up. The Stone Coat straightened her long legs, and off they went. "This isn't the path my grandmother took," cried the boy.

"Never mind," said the huge woman, "we will find her in a while." But the farther they went, the harder the boy cried, until finally the Stone Coat, getting hungry again, told him to climb down. The boy said no.

Being a Stone Coat, she could not get her hands

around to pull him off. Her arms were too stiff. She could not even turn her head to bite him. Knowing this, the boy clung to the middle of her back, realizing that she would eat him up if he slipped down. In this way they traveled on for a long while.

When the grandmother came home and saw that the boy and the girl were not there, she became uneasy. Finding the tracks of the Stone Coat around the lodge, she guessed what the trouble was. With a terrible roar she flew into the woods, sweeping up rocks and leaves as she sped along.

"Grandmother Whirlwind is on our trail," said the Stone Coat. "She will kill us both." The boy was silent.

Looking for a place to hide, the Stone Coat went into a deep ravine and dug a hole. Then she jumped in and let the dirt slip down around her until she was covered.

"Where are you?" cried the grandmother.

The Stone Coat lay still, whispering to the boy, "Be quiet." But the boy began to shout, and the grandmother, turning in the direction of his cries, blew off the earth from the hiding place and called to the boy, "Great Whirlwind! Get off!"

The boy jumped off and ran a short distance away, while the grandmother threw rocks, breaking the huge woman's clothes. When the Stone Coat lay dead, the

grandmother led the little boy home through the woods,
telling him, "Don't be afraid of Stone Coats. Remember, you, too, are a Whirlwind."

When they got to the lodge, the old woman lay down
on her bed. Then she said to her grandson, "Put me to
sleep." So the boy began to tell stories, and before he
was finished the grandmother was sleeping.

Soon a dream spirit came to her, and when she woke
up she cried, "A good word has come to me from my
dream being. We must go get your sister out of the
belly of the Stone Coat. She has been sitting there crying
for me all this time!"

Returning to the place where the Stone Coat lay, they built a fire, and the old woman began burning tobacco for her granddaughter, saying, "This is what we like. This is what we like." She burned half a pouch, fanning the smoke toward the Stone Coat, constantly saying, "This is what we like. Come out. Come out."

Suddenly the little girl jumped up and ran out through the Stone Coat's mouth, panting for breath, saying, "How long have I been here?" As they fanned the smoke, the little girl breathed from it until she regained her full strength. Then they all went home to their lodge.

But some of the Stone Coat people had found the trail of their sister, and when they came to where she lay and saw her clothes all broken, they started asking questions. As they talked, her spirit appeared and told them what had happened.

Not long after that, one of the Stone Coats arrived at Grandmother Whirlwind's lodge, talking pleasantly and asking how everyone was. Seeing that there were only three of them, the Stone Coat thought, "It will not be too much to finish them off."

As soon as the giant had left, the old woman said to her grandchildren, "We are in trouble now. The Stone Coats are coming to get us." Then she ran out of the lodge, calling, "Whirlwinds!"

"What do you mean?" asked the little girl.

"I am calling your relatives," the grandmother replied. "You are a Whirlwind, too."

One by one the Whirlwinds came. When sixty of them had gathered, they began to hear the enemy marching in the distance, thousands and thousands of them, coming down from the north. When the Stone Coats reached the river on the far side of the woods, they made a path of rocks across it and walked over without even wetting the soles of their moccasins.

Waiting for them, the Whirlwinds hid at the top of a high hill. For two days they camped there, listening to the war songs of the marching Stone Coats. On the evening of the third day the sound increased, and when the Stone Coats had all got into the valley below, the noise of their marching became a roar: dowowowowowow.

It grew louder and louder, until all of a sudden the Whirlwinds struck from both sides, throwing rocks and tearing trees out by the roots. The earth shook, and the hills on either side of the valley slid down on the giants. The sounds of their marching died out, and all that could be heard was the breaking and crashing of the trees. Only one Stone Coat was left alive, and he, although he escaped, was never seen again.

So there. I am through.

Animal-Foot Hitter

It is said that there were eight brothers living together. Their lodge was of bark and very long, with three fires down the middle.

The youngest of the brothers was a little boy who added nothing to the strength of the lodge, only providing another mouth to feed. While the others were out hunting, he would remain inside playing with a raccoon foot. Throwing it here, he would shoot at it, and throwing it there, he would shoot at it. He did not know what the light of outdoors was like.

When his brothers would leave in the morning, they would fasten the lodge securely and scatter ashes around the doorway, so that no one could pass without making telltale tracks. "Little brother," they would say, "you must not leave the lodge."

Now, there came a day when the oldest of the brothers returned from hunting without bringing anything, while the others had furs loaded with fresh meat. As they unpacked the skins and hung up the meat, the one who had nothing lay down on his bed and kept quiet.

It happened again the next day, and for many days it was the same. As usual, the youngest, who was still only an animal-foot hitter, remained behind.

While searching for game, the brothers always kept on the sun side. But at last the one who found nothing said, "This hunting ground is empty," and with these words he left the lodge, going north.

When he had traveled for some time, he began to see clear places in the forest, and just ahead lay a steep valley. As he was wondering which way to go, he heard a voice from deep in the valley saying, "Game has come to me. I can smell it."

At the same moment he heard the sound of a flicker, dot dot dot dot dot, and as he looked up, it smiled at him and said, "You couldn't hit anybody."

"Wah! I will kill you," said the hunter.

"Wa-a-ah! Your magic must be very great," replied the flicker.

Without wasting time, the young man strung his bow and shot an arrow. But it flew wide of the mark, sticking harmlessly in the tree trunk. Then he shot all of his arrows away, without troubling the flicker in the least.

Turning aside, he broke his bow and threw away the pieces. "That's that," he said, and he continued on until he reached the bottom of the valley. Looking around, he saw a lodge, with smoke rising. From inside came the voice of an old man: "My grandson, you have visited me."

As he went in, the hunter saw that the fire was a great one. He also saw a young woman seated on a mat, weaving strands of slippery-elm bark.

"Make room on your mat for our guest," said the old man. "You and he now become husband and wife. Prepare some food and set it before him. Use green corn as it cooks in the pot, and mix it with dried deer meat pounded fine, and add maple sugar and bear's fat to make it good."

When the hunter had eaten, the old sorcerer said, "Our guest is tired. Let him lie down, and I will tell my story." Then he began to sing:

> it is said
>
> there were eight brothers
>
> who lived in a lodge

This was the opening of his story, which he chanted three times. After a few moments, he shouted, "Are you listening?" The only reply was loud snoring.

"Why, the game animals come right into my lodge," cried the old man. Then he cut up the hunter's body, singing praises of himself as he put the pieces into a huge clay pot to cook. His voice continued to break forth as he went murmuring around the fire, saying, "This requires nothing but dumplings."

That evening, when the young man did not return, his brothers began to worry. The next morning the second oldest brother said, "I saw him yesterday starting toward the great valley." Then he strung up a bear's foot from the lodgepole so that it dangled over the fire, and after saying to the animal-foot hitter, "Here, have fun shooting this," he set out on his brother's trail.

In the evening the sky was red, and the remaining brothers knew that the one who had left in the morning had met the same fate as the one who had gone before. The next day, afraid to go north, the brothers started out to hunt as usual. The youngest sat by the fire, saying nothing.

When the others had left the lodge, he got up and took down his bow and arrows. Then he shot through the smoke hole, saying to the arrow, "Go for a large bear."

The brothers, who had not traveled far, were surprised to see a huge bear rush up to them and fall dead at their feet. Sticking out of its body was their little brother's arrow. When they returned to the lodge, carrying the meat, they found the little boy sitting by the fire. "Since our two missing brothers have not yet come home," he said, "I myself will have to go on their trail."

In the morning he ate no breakfast, so that his mind would be clear. As he sat by the fire, drinking medicine, he just straightened his arrows and strung his bow. Then he left the lodge, heading north.

When he got to the clear places, he found the tracks of his two brothers and heard the tapping of the flicker, as a voice from the valley said, "Fresh game has come to me." Then the flicker looked down at him and smiled, saying, "Animal-foot hitter, you couldn't kill anything."

A great many arrows were stuck in the tree near the spot where the bird was perched. The boy recognized them as his brothers' arrows. Then he aimed at the flicker and struck the very center of its body, pinning it to the tree.

Removing the arrow, with the bird still attached, he placed it on his shoulder and went on to the lodge at the bottom of the valley. As he came near, he heard a voice say, "My grandson, I am thankful that you have come to visit me." Entering, he saw the old sorcerer sitting next to a hot fire and the young woman on her mat, weaving.

"There sits my granddaughter, whom you are to

marry," said the old man. But in fact the young woman was a prisoner, too frightened to speak for herself. "Granddaughter, move over," the old man commanded, "and give your friend room to sit next to you."

As the boy passed alongside the fire, the sorcerer saw that he was carrying something, and he got up quickly, crying, "Give me the body of that thing you have shot."

"I will not give it up," said the boy. Furious, the old man pawed the earth like an animal and shouted until his throat bled.

"This bird contains your life," said the boy, "and I am your master, and you know it." Then he crushed the flicker's head with his war club, and the sorcerer fell to the ground like a tanned skin.

"You did not give me much trouble, though you called yourself powerful," said the boy. Then he turned to the young woman, and she led him to a place outside the lodge where the bones of his brothers lay scattered on the ground.

When the bones had been collected, the boy laid them under a tall elm tree and said, "You dry bones, watch out! A great elm is about to fall on those who sleep here. Brothers, arise!" At that moment the bones stood up as living men.

The brothers started for home, and the young woman, now free, went with them. When they had reached their own lodge and had greeted their remaining brothers, the youngest said, "We shall stay here in peace and contentment, for he who was in his time a mighty sorcerer has departed." And there in that lodge they live to this day.

That is the story.

Turtle's War Party

Do you believe old people who say Water runs day and night? Do you believe that Wind goes everywhere? Do you believe that trees grow? Don't be angry, I only want to know things. Do you believe the world rests on the Turtle's back?

Yes. Old people say it is true. But turtles have never done anything wonderful since the world began, and something you ought to know is that there was once a dissatisfied turtle who kept worrying about it. He said, "It is for me to show myself a leader of warriors and bring glory to the turtles." That's what he kept saying.

So, following his desire, he made the necessary preparations, got into his canoe, and paddled off down the river, singing:

> I am on the warpath
> I am on the warpath

When he had gone a short distance from his lodge, he saw someone running toward the river, calling out, "Friend, stop! I will go, too."

So Turtle stopped at the landing, and there on the bank stood Skunk. "I would like to go with you on the warpath," he said, and without asking questions Turtle told him to get into the canoe.

As he started off again, Turtle sang:

> I am on the warpath
> I am on the warpath
> you, brother, smell strong

They had not gone far when a voice called out, "Stop!" They made a landing and saw Porcupine. "What do you want?" they asked.

"I see you are on the warpath, and I want to go, too."

"Now, warrior," said Turtle, "show me your excellence."

Then Porcupine climbed onto a stump and shook himself, and his quills flew in all directions. "You'll do," said Turtle. "Get in."

Again they paddled off, with Turtle singing:

> I am on the warpath
> I am on the warpath
> you, brother, smell strong
> you, brother, have arrows

Hearing war songs, Rattlesnake called out from the bank, "Stop! I want to go, too."

"All right," said Turtle. "But first let me see you run. We are on our way to make war on the Seven Sisters, and we can only take swift runners. Now, run to that mountain over there as fast as you can and come right back."

Rattlesnake raised his head and got ready to run. But Turtle looked at him and said, "Never mind. You'll do. You are my warrior."

As they all started off, Turtle was singing:

I am on the warpath

I am on the warpath

you, brother, smell strong

you, brother, have arrows

you, brother, have black face

They paddled on until it was nearly night. Then they landed the canoe at a spot not far from the lodge of the Seven Sisters.

As they started through the woods, Turtle took the lead, and they asked him, "What sort of thing does your body pretend to be as it flies along?"

Turtle replied, "Oh, just the night owl, saying wu, wu, wu, wu, hu, hu-u."

"Ha!" cried the others. "You are a brave male!"

"And what will you be?" asked Turtle.

"As for ourselves, we will be foxes and just go along barking," they said.

"I will hear you," said Turtle, and in this way they approached the lodge where the Seven Sisters were sleeping. When they arrived, Skunk positioned himself next to the fire pit. Porcupine climbed into the woodpile, and Rattlesnake hid in the skin bucket where the shelled corn was kept, whispering that he would attack the first person who came in the morning for corn.

Meanwhile, Turtle hid under the rocks at the spring.

Just at dawn the mother of the Seven Sisters got up and began to stir the fire. Skunk immediately attacked her with his odor. "Ik!" she cried.

Hearing the commotion, the sisters all jumped out of bed and fell on Skunk. They beat his head flat with their fists. Then one of them reached for firewood and found her hand shot full of quills. The others picked up sticks from the woodpile, clubbed Porcupine, and threw his body out the door.

When it was time to grind meal for making the day's bread, one of the sisters went to the corn bucket, and just as she got there, she saw Rattlesnake coiled among the kernels. But before he had a chance to strike, she dropped a heavy stone on him, and there he stayed.

After that, the old mother asked one of her daughters to bring water from the spring. The daughter went. But as she was stooping down to draw up the water, Turtle bit her toe and held on. She could not get him off and had to walk backward, dragging him along.

When her mother saw her coming, she shouted, "Throw him into the fire and let him burn up."

Turtle laughed and said, "Fire is my natural home, and I am lonesome. Hurry up and put me there."

The old woman changed her mind. "Here, let me take

him to the creek," she said. "We'll drown him."

Turtle cried out, "Oh no! I would die!" He begged so hard that the mother and all the sisters caught hold of him and dragged him to the water as fast as they could and threw him in.

Laughing to himself, Turtle swam underwater until he was out of danger, then reappeared and floated comfortably down the creek. But he was discouraged. "No," he thought, "I am not a great chief."

He kept thinking. At last he said, "But I am a turtle and am satisfied. The glory of turtles is that the earth and all creation rests on the back of one."

This is the length of the story.

The Mother of Ghosts

In a certain country there stood a lodge surrounded by thick woods, and in this lodge lived a very old man and his seven sons. Only the youngest had a name—Bright Body.

This small boy and his tiny dog, which was no bigger than a gray squirrel, played together every day, hunting fleas around the fire pit. The dog would track a flea, and just as the flea would leap up from its hiding place, the boy would shoot it with an arrow from his tiny bow. In this way he kept himself busy all day and far into the night.

Now, the father of this family had forbidden his sons to go hunting in a certain direction from the lodge. But one by one they disobeyed him, and each in turn vanished from sight. Finally the old man set out to find them, and as he, too, failed to return, Bright Body was left by himself.

The time was winter, but the little boy knew he would have to leave. After slapping his dog three times with a red-willow switch, causing it to become large, he sent it off to care for itself. Then he started out on the trail of his father and brothers.

He had no provisions to eat on the way, but he traveled on until the darkness made it difficult for him to go farther. When it was quite dark, he came to a rough shelter formed by the interlocking limbs of fallen trees, which held the snow so as to make a kind of roof.

Inside, he found that the place was dry, and there he decided to spend the night. Although he had no food to cook, he kindled a fire with twigs, and as the heat began to spread, a covey of quail came out from under the branches that formed the shelter.

Stringing his bow, he shot a few of the birds and cooked them over the fire. After he had eaten, he settled down for the night, burrowing into the dry leaves.

The next morning, an old woman who lived not far away left her lodge to get hickory bark to keep up her fire. Noticing smoke coming up through the snow, she went to investigate and was astonished to discover a small boy under the snow-covered branches. Moved by pity, she took him home and placed before him what little food she had, saying that she wanted him to live with her as her grandchild.

The day after that, when all the food was gone, the boy licked his fingers and rubbed one of his arrows three times. Then he shot it up through the smoke hole, saying to it, "Go! Hunt for a deer and kill it for our food."

Obeying him, the arrow flew out of the smoke hole, and after a while it came back on its own, carrying traces of fresh blood. "Grandmother," said the boy, "go out and look for the body of a deer. It lies not far from here." The old woman soon found the deer, and when she saw it, she uttered words of thanksgiving to the Master of Life.

Every day after that, the boy sent his arrow out to hunt for food. In this way the old woman and her grandchild lived for several years, and the boy grew to manhood.

One day the chief of the village announced that the best hunter among all the young men would be given his daughter as a prize. Then all the young hunters set out to find deer and bear, and the old woman's grandson joined them.

With his magic arrow the grandson killed twenty-four deer, while the others got five or six apiece. The chief examined the deer, then told the young man to go to the long lodge and claim his bride.

But when the other hunters learned that the old woman's grandson had won the prize, they were jealous. Secretly they hired a sorcerer, who agreed to pierce the young man's heart with a bark splinter just at day-break.

So it happened that the young man died in his wife's arms at dawn of the next day. Stricken with grief, the young woman walked outside to see whether the sun had come up, so that she could start mourning without disturbing her husband's spirit.

At that moment she heard the door, which she had just closed after her, open, and looking back, she saw her husband come out of the lodge and walk quickly past her without speaking. She followed him as best she could, but she could not quite overtake him. For three days and three nights she kept on his trail, never tiring and never becoming hungry.

At dawn on the fourth day she suddenly came to a narrow passage, where a man stood guard. He blocked her path, saying, "What brings you to this place, seeing that you are not dead? This is not the land of the living."

She quickly answered him, "I am following the tracks of my husband."

The guard seemed not to be satisfied. But when she told him all that had happened, he decided to help her.

"You must take with you this gourd, which is closed with a stopper," he said. "In it you will have to bring back the soul of your husband, tightly closed up. You

must also take this small gourd, which contains the oil of man. When you get to a large strawberry field, stretching on both sides of the path, rub some of the oil on the palms of your hands. In this field you will see an old woman, picking berries. Show her your hands. She is the Mother of Ghosts, and she will help you with everything."

The young wife continued down the path. When she came to the strawberry field, she rubbed the oil on the palms of her hands and held them out in front of her. "What are you doing here?" asked the old woman. "You are not dead."

"I am looking for my husband, whose trail comes here."
As she spoke, she gave the large gourd to the Mother
of Ghosts.

The old woman looked at it carefully, then replied,
"Very well, I will put your husband into the gourd, so
that you may take him back with you. Come now to my
lodge."

Once inside, the old woman hid her guest behind some
pieces of bark that were stacked in a corner. When night
came, the ghosts entered one by one, and the mother
began to sing and beat on a drum. From her hiding
place the young woman could hear the ghosts dancing.

After a short while, the dancers said, "What is this?
We smell the odor of a human being." Then they started
to run from the room.

But the mother scolded them, saying, "Wah! It is only
I that you smell, for I am now getting very old again."
So they did not leave the room but continued dancing.

When the ghost of the newly arrived husband passed
close to the mother, she seized him, and as the other
dancers fled from the room, she pressed him into the
gourd and closed it up with the stopper. Then she handed
it to the young woman, saying, "Go now! Be quick, or
they will try to stop you. The man at the passageway
will tell you what to do."

Hurrying from the lodge into the darkness, the young wife again found the trail and soon reached the narrow passageway. The guard said to her, "When you arrive at your home, you must open the gourd into your husband's mouth. But first you must close up his nose, his ears, and every opening of his body, so that his life cannot escape."

Having understood these instructions, the young woman went on, traveling for three days and three nights. As soon as she reached home, she prepared her husband's body as she had been told to do, filling every opening and outlet with fine clay mixed with deer fat to soften it. Then she rubbed him with the oil of man and opened the gourd into his mouth. In a few moments he came back to life.

After that the body of the husband was safe from the spells and charm words of sorcerers. For many years the good wife and her husband lived together in peace, until finally, at an old age, they died and went home again to the Mother of Ghosts.

I am now through with what I have to say.

Cannibal Island

My grandfather used to tell it to go to sleep by.

It is said there was a boy named Rooted, who lived in the woods with his uncle, Planter. The uncle had a great elm tree in front of his lodge, and Rooted, the nephew, lay at the foot of this tree, its roots growing over and around his body, holding him to the earth.

One spring morning, while the uncle was off in the field planting seeds, he heard the song, "I am rising, I am rising." Dropping his seeds, he ran to the elm tree and saw that his nephew was resting on one elbow and that the tree was beginning to lean.

"I am thirsty," said the boy.

The uncle gave him some water, then pushed the tree back to an upright position and returned to his planting. Again he heard the nephew's song, "I am rising, I am rising."

"Poor boy, I wonder what he wants now," said the uncle. When he was halfway home, there came a tremendous crash, which was heard over the whole country.

All the people said, "Rooted has come to manhood. He has stood up."

That night the young man and his uncle had a talk. "You are grown," said the old man. "You can go where you please. But don't go west. There are evil things in the world reaching from the bottom of the water up to the home of the Master of Life."

The next day the young man turned his back on the morning and headed west. He had not gone far when he came to a lodge at the edge of a large lake. An old man invited him in, saying, "The first thing for us to do will be to eat together." He had a pot of corn and beans with plenty of bear's meat for seasoning. When they had eaten, he said, "Now is our time. We will go hunting on the little island."

Then they got into the old man's canoe, which was pushed by two rows of geese, one on each side. The old man sang, "Now wild geese's feet, row my canoe," and they sailed over the water.

When they had touched land, they separated to hunt for game. But as Rooted walked into the woods, he heard the old man's song again and, turning around, saw him sailing back to the mainland. Then he heard him call out to the creatures in the lake, "If the man on the island tries to swim, eat him at once," and great hoarse voices out of the water answered, "We will."

As the young man was watching the canoe disappear

over the lake, he heard a voice near him saying, "My nephew, come to me." Surprised, he turned around and walked to the spot where the sound was coming from. There he saw a pile of bones covered with moss. "A cannibal is coming tonight to eat you," said the bones, "but do me a favor, and I will tell you how to save yourself. Go over to that tree and dig up my pouch, so I can smoke."

The young man found the pouch and lit the pipe for his uncle, the bones. As the uncle inhaled, smoke escaped from the nose and eye openings, and the mice that had been living inside the skull came running out. "Ah, that feels better," said the bones.

"Now you must cut red willow and make stick men, and bows and arrows to put in their hands. Set them up in the woods," said the bones, "then hide under the cliff at the far end of the island. No one can find you there." Then the young man did as he was told.

When evening came, the cannibal landed with three dogs, all yelping and barking, wow wow wow wow wow. Turning them loose, he cried, "Chwa! Go, my servants, and find my food." But one by one the dogs were shot by the stick men.

"Oh, this is discouraging," said the cannibal, and he got back into his canoe and paddled away.

The next morning, as the young man came out from his hiding place, he heard the voice from the bones calling for a smoke, and when he had lit the pipe, the uncle began to talk once more. "Now, I have something to tell you," he said. "You have a sister who was brought to this country long ago. The cannibal took her to his own lodge on the mainland. You must go there and rescue her."

As he spoke, the sound of the old man and his geese

could be heard coming over the water. Rooted ran and hid as they pushed to shore. Then the old man climbed out of the canoe and headed for the woods, saying to himself, "Let me see if my grandson has spilled his blood." When he was out of sight, Rooted jumped into the canoe, singing, "Now wild geese's feet, row me home."

Terrified, the old man ran back to the shore. "Let me get aboard, let me get aboard!" he cried. But Rooted just spoke to the water, saying, "If he tries to swim after me, eat him," and up from the depths came a confusion of voices saying, "It shall be done, it shall be done."

Reaching the mainland, the young man ran the canoe aground and gave the geese their freedom. Not far from the shore stood the cannibal's lodge, and in the doorway he saw a woman waiting for him.

When they were inside the lodge together, he said to the woman, "I have come for you. I am your brother."

She replied, "I will go with you as soon as it is safe. You must hide now." Under her bed was a smaller one, in which she put her brother. Then she replaced her own bed over it and sat down on top.

At this time the cannibal was just returning to the island with three new dogs. In a moment the dogs had tracked the old man, who was shouting, "I am your servant! I am your servant!" But the cannibal did not believe him, and when he had shot him, he ate him, throwing his bones into the woods.

With the blood still on his mouth, the cannibal paddled back across the water and returned to his lodge. As he sat down by the fire, he said, "Now I shall take a smoke." Soon he added, "My niece has two ways of breathing."

Understanding his words, the woman protested, "Oh, no. I am alone."

"There is game in the lodge," said the cannibal.

"I told you I am alone," she insisted.

"Its fresh trail comes in at the door," he said.

"Well, perhaps it came in and went off another way."

The cannibal walked outside to look around. While he was gone, the woman and her brother slipped out the other door and ran to the canoe.

Climbing aboard, the two paddled away as quickly as possible. They had gone only a short distance, however, when they heard the cannibal shouting, "You cannot escape me, you cannot escape me!" Unwinding a fishline, the cannibal threw the hook, saying to it, "Catch the canoe."

With a jerk the canoe stopped and began to speed backward. But the woman picked up a hatchet that was lying in the bottom of the canoe and broke the line.

Then the cannibal lay down on the shore and began drinking the water of the lake. He drank so fast that the water ran toward him in a great stream. His mouth was enormous, and his body grew bigger and bigger as the lake poured into him, drawing the canoe along with it.

Taking good aim, the young man shot an arrow into the huge belly, causing it to give out a sound, bu! And the water bursting forth through the wound sent the canoe flying back toward the far shore.

Paddling on, the two reached the place where the lodge stood that had belonged to the cannibal's old servant. Beaching the canoe, they traveled on without stopping. And how did they find their way? Oh! They followed the bend of the hemlocks. The tops of the trees lean toward the east.

When they arrived at the lodge of the old uncle, Planter, the young man said to his sister, "My sister! You were so small when you went away! But this is your home, too, because I know now that Planter is your uncle as well as mine."

Entering, they found the uncle eating his midday meal. He quickly arose and seized the young man, saying, "Have you returned? Is it you, my nephew? Are you Rooted?"

The nephew answered, "It is I."

After this the young man began to hunt, so that his uncle and sister would be comfortable, and he made their days easy with soft beds and much meat.

This is the end of the story.

The Moose Wife

A young man living alone with his mother decided to go into the woods to hunt for a whole year, collecting and drying meat. He walked for many days until he came to a place where there were deer and other game, and after building a cabin, he began living by himself.

Every day he would make a fire, get breakfast, and set off to hunt. He would stay away all day. When he got home at night he would be too tired to make supper and would just throw himself on his bed and fall asleep. He was collecting a great quantity of cured meat.

One evening, as he was returning to his cabin, he saw smoke coming out through the smoke hole in the roof. Thinking the fire he had made that morning must some-how have spread, he began to run. But when he got inside, he was surprised to see a nice fire burning in the fire pit and his kettle, already boiled, hanging on the crook just close enough to keep it warm.

He sat down and ate the supper, saying in his mind, "Surely the person who got this ready will come back." But no one came.

The next evening he again found supper ready. As he ate, he looked around and noticed a braid of bark fibers and knew that a woman had been at work. Thinking how kind she was, he made up his mind to see her.

In the morning he set off as though he were going to hunt but went only a short way into the woods. He had built no fire that morning so he would be able to tell when fresh smoke started rising. The moment it appeared, he began retracing his steps, and as he crept through the trees, he saw a young woman come out of the cabin and pick up an armful of wood.

When she went back inside, he followed as quickly as possible. She saw him, and he said to her, "You have been good to me."

She replied, "I knew you were starving for lack of a woman's help, so I came to see whether you would take me as your wife."

He accepted her offer, and from then on she never left him. Every day she made his supper. She tanned his deerskins. When pieces of firewood were ready, she would carry them inside, and as she would throw them down, they would make a deep, pleasant sound on the earth.

Before the end of a year a boy was born to them, and they were perfectly happy. When the time came for him to visit his mother, his wife said to him, "I know you must go. Here, I have made moccasins for you and your mother," and she handed him two wrapped bundles.

She knew how he had come, but she knew he would return more quickly if he followed the river. Reaching into her dress, she took out a tiny canoe and told him to pull one end. As he pulled, it became full-sized. Then together they brought deerskins and basketfuls of meat and packed everything away in the canoe.

"I will stay here," she said. "But when you get to the village, people will find out that you have brought all kinds of meat and skins. Someone will come to you and say, 'You must marry my daughter.' An old woman will

say, 'You must marry my granddaughter.' But do not listen to them. Remain true to me."

He gave his promise and started off. When he reached his mother's lodge, the news spread that a certain woman's son had returned from a year's hunting, and people came to see what he had brought. There were young girls who asked for him as a husband, but he refused to look at them.

After a while he said to his mother, "I am going to the woods again. I have a cabin there, and someday you will know why I do not wish to marry."

When he got to the river, he shook the little boat, as his wife had told him to do, and it again stretched out. After a long journey he came to the landing near his cabin and saw his wife waiting for him and his little boy playing on the bank.

Another year passed. They had all the meat they could take care of, and another boy had been born to them.

Again his wife got him ready to carry meat to his mother, just as she had done the year before, saying, "You must be true to me, and I will be true to you."

"Very well," he said, "I do not want my mind to be different from yours."

But something worried her. "If you marry another woman," she said, "you will never see me again. Remember me and your children. If you do not, your hunting power will vanish and your new wife will soon be sucking her moccasins from hunger." He promised her everything.

When he reached his old home, he found that his fame as a hunter had spread to many villages. Beautiful young women came to ask for him, and his mother repeatedly urged him to marry. Still he resisted.

One day an old woman of the Snake people, living in a distant village, called to the oldest of her granddaughters and began speaking to her. This old woman was the head woman of her tribe. She had two snakes tattooed on her lips—the upper jaws of the snakes were on her upper lip, the lower jaws on her lower lip. When she opened her mouth, the snakes seemed to open theirs.

As she talked to her granddaughter, she rubbed the girl's hair with fine-smelling bear grease and braided it very close, wrapping the braids so tight that the girl seemed not to have any eyebrows left. "You must go to the good hunter's village," she told her. "You must find out whether he will marry you."

When the Snake woman's granddaughter reached the young man's village, she went directly to his mother's lodge. Fascinated by her beauty, and worn down by his mother's urging, the young man at last said yes.

At that moment the wife in the woods, knowing what had happened, said, "Children, we must be getting ready to go away. Your father does not love us and will never come back." She was weeping as she made her preparations.

Now, after the young man had taken a second wife, the meat in his lodge began to get smaller. He could almost see it shrinking, and in a few days it was gone. He went hunting, but the animals did not come to him. Their trails had disappeared.

One day, when he came home, he found his new wife sucking her moccasins. Seeing how hungry she was, he prayed to the stars, the moon, and the sun for hunting luck. But none came. He cried to the Good Minded Spirit until it seemed that the prayer was only like hollow talking in his throat.

Then he remembered his wife and children and thought, "This is my punishment," and without saying a word to anyone he set out.

After a long journey he reached his old cabin. Not a single footprint was to be seen by the door. He went inside and found the cabin empty. He was hungry, but there was no food. He saw nothing but three small bundles of ashes next to the fire pit. They were of different sizes, and the third was very small.

He thought for a moment, then knew that this was a sign, left by his wife in case he should return. After wondering for some time, he realized that the three bundles meant he had three children now, and he made up his mind to follow them.

He thought, "My boys are playful. As they went along, they must have hacked the trees." Walking into the woods, he found marks on the trees, and in this way he was able to trace his family.

After a day's journey he found the remains of a fire, where his wife and children had camped for the night. The next day he walked on and found the remains of another fire.

About noon of the following day he saw smoke in the distance and came to a cabin. Hungry and tired, he thought he would ask for food. Inside he found two small boys and a woman whose back was turned as she tended the fire.

The older boy, recognizing his father, ran to him and put his hand on his knee. But the father did not realize it was his son and gently pushed him away.

At that moment the mother turned around and said, "You see? He does not love you."

Recognizing his wife, the man cried out to her, pleading with her to take him back. He begged so hard that at last she forgave him and showed him his little daughter, born after he had gone away.

From that time on he was true to his Moose wife—for she was a Moose woman—and he never again left his home in the woods.

The Boy Who Learned the Songs of Birds

Two brothers living by themselves in a quiet forest believed that they were the only people in the world. They were very fond of each other.

The younger brother was just a little boy, it seems, but he did the thinking and the planning for both. Whatever he would say his older brother would do.

One day he pointed to the woods and said, "Brother, go kill me a turkey. I want its feathers."

"I will," answered the brother, and he went directly to the place that was being pointed to and brought back the turkey.

The younger boy then plucked just two of the feathers and, using a chin strap, attached them to his head. This made him look more important.

The next morning the little boy went into the woods by himself. His older brother watched from a distance and saw him go behind a fallen tree. When he returned, the brother said, "What were you doing? Weren't you dancing? Why don't you dance here in the lodge, so that I can dance with you?"

"But you don't know the songs I sing," said the little brother. "It's because I shoot birds, and they're the ones who teach me my songs. You shoot larger animals that don't sing."

From that time on, the boy studied the songs of birds, and he grew wise. He became experienced in the ways of magic. Day after day he would say, "These are the songs that people will sing in future times, and they, too, will wear feathers on their heads."

In the evening when the two brothers would come home from hunting, they would always eat their supper together. One night, however, the older boy, when he returned to the lodge, could not find his little brother. He ate alone, then went to bed.

In the morning he heard his brother on the roof making the noises that turkeys make at daybreak. This caused the older brother to feel very strange. Soon he heard the turkey brother jump to the ground and run to the door of the lodge.

"Brother, brother!" cried the little boy. "Two women are coming. I think they want to see you." In a moment two women appeared from the west, sailing in a canoe through the air.

"Where is he?" they cried. "Your brother, where is he?"

"He is off hunting," said the little boy.

"There is someone here with you in the lodge," said one of the women, sniffing the air, and in a fascinating voice that thrilled the heart of the older brother, she said, "We have come to bring him home with us."

"He isn't here," cried the little boy. "I'm all by myself."

But his older brother was already standing at the door. "I must go with them," he said. "Their power is greater than ours." Quickly he took his place between the two women, and the canoe, becoming alive, rushed into the air, headed west.

The turkey brother was now alone. Toward evening he felt very lonely and spent the night worrying. In the morning he said to himself, "Oh, my poor brother. If anything happens to him, I will dream about it!" Then came the thought, "I must go after him."

Reaching into his shirt, he drew out a tiny black dog, and pulling its ears and shaking it gently, he said the words: "Grow, my dog! Grow, my dog!" All at once the dog increased in size, becoming as large as a bear.

The boy and the dog listened. They heard no sound. They listened again. Then the boy said, "I hear my brother. It must be that he is crying in the far west."

The dog growled and said, "Put on new moccasins

and take along a second pair. I will lick the soles of your feet to give you speed."

The dog licked the soles of the boy's feet, and the boy put on the new moccasins. Then together they set off so rapidly that only the wind could be heard flowing past them.

Just at dark they arrived at the edge of a large clearing. In the center stood a long lodge and nearby, close to the woods, a small hut. Holding the dog by the ears, the boy shook it until it grew small again, then he put it back inside his shirt. As he did this, he thought, "I will go over to the little hut."

An old woman was living there. When the boy got to the door, he said, "Grandmother, may I stay with you tonight?"

"Oh, grandchild," said the old woman, "I have so little to give. I am alone and poor."

"All I want is a place to stay," said the boy. "I do not want food." Then he began to question her. She told him, "There is a great gathering at the long lodge. The chief's two daughters have brought a young man from the east. They hung him up last night and made him cry. His tears are wampum beads. Tonight they will do the same thing."

The boy was angry. When he heard shouts coming

from the middle of the village, he said, "I am going over to the long lodge."

Arriving at the entrance, he pretended to be only a little boy playing around with the other children who were going inside. As he entered, the chief was just standing up, saying, "Now, all be ready. Look out for the beads."

His two daughters were lighting torches for the people who were about to burn the prisoner's feet. The torches were lit and held under first one foot and then the other. As the tears began to flow from the young man's eyes, they turned to wampum, falling in a shower. All the people ran to collect the beads. Then they rested awhile and smoked.

When the order was given to start again, fresh torches were lit, and again the young man wept tears of wampum. But this time, while the people were on their knees picking up the beads, the little boy rushed forward, untied his brother, and led him outside.

The younger boy then called in a loud voice:

> you are coming
> you brave ones
> my guardian spirits
> you small hummingbirds

Running round and round the lodge, he continued to shout, saying, "Let no one escape, no matter how great a wizard he or she may be. Let the top and the bottom and the sides of the lodge be closed up, and let the lodge be red-hot. Be strong, my spirits, be strong."

The hummingbirds came to his aid, making the sound dow-w-w-w as they worked. Suddenly the lodge burst into flames. Inside, the people screamed. Slowly the sounds they made as they tried to escape died away.

Then the little boy said to his brother, "Let's go home." But the brother's feet had been so badly burned he could hardly walk.

So the turkey brother reached into his shirt, and saying, "Come to me, Beautiful Ears," he pulled out the tiny dog and shook it until it grew to its full size. With the older boy riding on the dog's back and his little brother running alongside, they set out toward the east and soon returned to their own lodge.

When they got there, the little boy scolded his older brother, saying, "You caused me a lot of trouble. I told you not to go with those women, but you would not listen. Now you have had your punishment. But I am glad you are back home. We are free again and can live happily together from now on."

My story has ended.

Turtle Goes Hunting

Here is another one.

Two brothers, Partridge and Turtle, lived together. Wolves, their cousins, lived in a house not far away. One day old man Wolf said, "Our food supplies are getting low. You young ones had better go hunting."

So they all went into the woods, single file, after saying, "Whoever sees game will give a shout." Turtle was slow and fell behind. But in a while he gave a shout.

Partridge came running. "Where is it?" he said. "What did you find?"

"It's this log," said Turtle. "It's too high. I can't climb over it."

"Don't shout again unless you find game," said Partridge, and picking Turtle up by the leg, he threw him over the log.

After a while Turtle shouted again, louder this time.

"What is it? What is it?" cried Partridge.

"Another log," said Turtle. "A high one."

"Just go around it," said Partridge.

"I can't. We're going in single file."

Then Partridge picked him up by the leg and threw him over as hard as he could. After that, Turtle went around the logs. In a while he came to a river, and near the river he saw a tree loaded with plums. Some of the plums had fallen to the ground.

Turtle had on a bark apron. He gathered the apron, bag shape, and filled it with plums. While he was eating and looking around, he saw Elk coming.

"Brother," said Elk, "will you give me some plums?"

"No," said Turtle, "I'm small, and it's too hard for me to knock them off the tree."

"How do you knock them off the tree?"

"Run up to it as fast as you can and hit it with your head."

But when Elk hit the tree, it threw him back and he couldn't get up. Turtle dropped his plums and jumped on Elk, caught him by the neck, and choked him to death. Then he gave out with a loud shout.

Partridge came running up. "What have you done now?" he said.

"I'm a man. I've killed an elk."

Partridge was glad. "Well," he said, "how can we hide this from our cousins? They're great eaters and would finish it up. But you and I are small people. We could live on it a long time."

"If we could find a hollow tree, we could hide the meat there," said Turtle.

"I'll look for the tree," said Partridge. "You go find our cousins and borrow their knife. If they ask why, tell them you need it to dig mushrooms."

"No," said Turtle, "you go, because you can fly. If I go, they'll track me and find out what we're doing. If they ask why you need the knife, tell them you have to give me a haircut."

Partridge flew over to where the Wolves were hunting. The first thing they asked was whether he had had any luck. Partridge tried to answer, but he began to stutter and couldn't get out a single word.

"What makes you stutter?" asked the cousins. "You're scared! Have you done something bad?"

Partridge tried to speak but couldn't. All he could do was point to the knife. "Is this what you want?" they asked. "Well, take it."

Partridge took the knife, and when he got back to where Turtle was, they cut up the meat and carried it piece by piece to a hollow tree that Turtle had found. Then they camped in the tree.

For two changes of the moon they lived there. When cold weather came, the Wolves began wondering where their cousins were. Looking in all directions, they at last saw smoke coming out of a hollow tree, and when they got up close, they saw bones lying all around. Partridge had told Turtle not to throw the bones out, because the Wolves would smell them, but he had done it anyway.

When the Wolves smelled the bones, they were furious. Before this the cousins had always shared their meat. "Let's cut down the tree," they said.

They set to work, and soon the tree began to bend over. Frightened, Turtle asked Partridge, "Can you carry me in your shirt?"

"Maybe I can, if you hold on tight."

Partridge flew off, and Turtle hung inside his shirt until he was too tired to hold on any longer. Then he

fell, and the Wolves, who had followed, said, "Now we'll get him."

"What will we do with him?" asked one. "Roast him?"

"You can roast me," said Turtle, "but you'll never have a fire again. I'll put it out forever."

"Maybe he could do that," said the Wolves. "Let's chop him to pieces."

"You can if you want to," said Turtle, "but you'll never have a sharp knife again. My back is made of bone."

"That's true," said the Wolves.

"Here's how we can kill him," said one. "Drag him to the lake and throw him in!"

Turtle began to cry and beg, saying, "I'll die if you throw me into the water."

He cried so hard that they believed him. Satisfied, they dragged him to the lake, threw him in, then sat down on the shore to watch him drown.

But Turtle stuck his head up, and seeing the Wolves, who remained on the shore, he called out, "You fools! Didn't you know that water is my home?" And so it is.

Well, it was at this time that partridges, wolves, and turtles stopped being people and became what they are today. That's all I have to say. The story is ended.

Mother Swan's Daughters

There was an old woman of the Swan people whose three daughters had grown to young womanhood. One day she said to them, "My daughters, I have had a great deal of trouble bringing you up, and so far I have eaten nothing but mushrooms. Now I would like to have some meat to eat. There is a rich woman of the Eagle people, named Big Earth, who has a son, Long Face. He is a good young man and a great hunter. I want two of you to go to her lodge and marry this son."

The girls began at once to make the marriage bread. They boiled the flour corn in ashes and washed the grains in clean water. With a cry of "Come now," they set to work pounding the corn into meal. The sounds made by their wooden corn pounders were tut, tut, tut, tut, tut. It was not long before they had prepared the twenty loaves that were needed.

As soon as the bread had been placed in a basket, the mother said to the oldest daughter, "Come to me." The girl obeyed her, and the mother set to work dressing her hair. Then she dressed the hair of the second oldest and handed the basket of marriage bread to the two sisters, saying, "Stop nowhere until you come to the lodge of Big Earth, and do not ask directions of anyone on the way or speak to any man." The older daughter took the basket, and her younger sister followed.

About noon they saw a man of the Owl people running across the road. He was saying, "I lost my arrow. I was shooting a squirrel in a tree, and my arrow went so far I can't find it."

The older daughter put her basket on a log, and both girls began hunting for the arrow. The younger girl did not like to do this and repeated out loud what their mother had told them, but still she had to follow her older sister. While the girls were looking for the arrow, the Owl man slipped behind them and ran off with the marriage bread.

Returning to the log and finding their basket gone, the two sisters went directly home. When their mother asked them what had happened, the younger said, "A man told us to look for his arrow, and I think he stole our bread."

The old woman scolded them, saying, "You do not love me. You know that I am suffering for meat, and still you disobey me." Then she said to the younger girl, "We will make more marriage bread tomorrow, and you

and your younger sister will go for the young man."

The next day they made another twenty loaves. The day after, the mother dressed the girls' hair and said to the youngest, "If your sister wants to stop, make her go on."

The sisters set out. After traveling awhile they met the same old Owl man. "Don't speak to him," warned the younger girl, remembering her mother's words. But as they came up to him, he was so kind and pleasant that the sister asked, "How far is it to Big Earth's lodge?"

"Oh," he said, "it is not so far." And pointing to his own lodge, he said, "It is right over there." In his mind he was thinking, "I will marry these girls myself." But already he had a wife and one little boy.

Running around to the lodge, he told his wife to go to the other side of the fire with her child. Then he threw ashes over her to make her look old, telling her to pretend that he was her brother. She obeyed him.

Soon the two girls came in, and as the old man had painted himself to look young, they sat down beside him, thinking he must be the young man they had come for. After a few moments the little boy began to say, "Father! Father!" But Owl explained, "This is my sister's son. His father was buried yesterday, and the boy is calling for him." Then Owl pretended to cry tears for his brother-in-law.

At last somebody was heard running. The person came and kicked at the door, calling, "Owl, they want you at Big Earth's long lodge." Owl said to the girls, "They are always using nicknames here. My real name is Long Face. They are holding a council and cannot get along without me, so I must go. Lie down whenever you are tired, and I will come home soon." Then off he went to the council.

The younger girl whispered, "Let us go out. This isn't Long Face. It's the man we met on the way, and mother told us not to speak to anyone."

"I suppose we have done wrong," said her sister. Then

they put two rotten logs in the bed and, after covering them up, started on with their basket of marriage bread.

Soon they came to an open place where a council lodge stood. They could hear sounds of laughter. Peeping in, they saw Owl in the middle of the floor and people singing for him to dance. As he danced, they threw mush into his mouth and hit his blanket with lumps of fat. He was a sight to look at. The girls recognized him and thought to themselves, "His mind is not strong."

A woman and her son sat by the fire, and these two looked very attractive. The younger sister whispered, "That is the young man we want."

Entering the lodge, they walked up to the old woman, Big Earth, and put down the basket. Big Earth was pleased. The dancing was now over, and all the people were going home. Foolish Owl, his dance finished, went out, too.

Then Big Earth placed the bread in front of her son and said, "Eat. These young women have come to marry you." He thanked them and ate the bread, and with that they were married.

Meanwhile Owl returned to his own lodge. Seeing what he thought were the two young women lying in his bed, he said, "Well, I must smoke. They had a big council over there, but they couldn't do anything. Oh, I tried to help them."

Taking down a piece of deer tallow, he chewed it, and every time he spat, it simmered on the fire. As he smoked, he chewed and spat and chewed and spat, and the fat in the fire kept simmering.

As he was sitting there, he was bitten by a black ant. Thinking one of the girls had pinched him, he said, "Don't be impatient. I will be there soon." At last, having finished his smoke, he lay down and discovered the two rotten logs and a bed full of ants. Furious, he scolded his wife for letting the girls escape and threw the logs out the door.

For two months thereafter the girls lived happily with Big Earth's son. At the end of that time, Big Earth said to them, "You must go home now and take your mother some meat. She is suffering for it, I know."

Putting many pieces of meat together, she tied the whole pile with bark ropes, then shook it, saying, "I want you to be small." Immediately it shrank to a small bundle, which she handed to the young women. Before they left, she said, "You must bring your mother here. I will give her one fire in the lodge for her own use."

When the girls arrived at their old home, they shook the meat again, and it regained its former size. Mother Swan ate until her jaws could move no longer and her tongue refused to stir. Having eaten enough, she was glad.

Then her daughters brought her to Big Earth's lodge, where she lived happily, and her mind was contented at last.

So that is the story.

Lodge Boy and Thrown Away

In a miserable old lodge in the woods a father and a mother were living together with their little boy. When the boy was still small, the mother gave birth to a second son, not longer than a hand's length. This tiny baby was bright and lively. But the father, thinking so small a child could not live, wrapped him up and placed him in a hollow tree outside the lodge. Then he burned the body of the mother, who had died when the baby was born.

The next day the man went hunting, as usual, and while he was gone, the older boy played by himself in the lodge. Without his mother he was lonely. Suddenly he heard the baby in the hollow log crying. The baby was lonely, too, and had nothing to eat.

Then the lodge boy went and found his little brother and, making a soup of deer intestines, gave it to him to drink. Finally the tiny child came out of the log and the two brothers played together. The older brother fixed the little one a coat of fawn skin and put it on him. It made him look like a chipmunk as he ran around the fire.

When the father came home, he said, "What happened to the deer intestines?"

"Oh," said the boy, "I ate quite a lot of them."

Looking around the fire, the father saw a tiny track with very short steps. "Whose is it?" he asked. The boy was silent. Then, finally, he told his father how he had found the little brother and had given him soup.

"Go and bring him in," said the father.

"He would be too timid to come" was the answer.

"Well, we will catch him."

The father went out to the hollow tree, reached in, and picked up the little boy. The child screamed and struggled, but it was no use. He could not get away. To please him, the father put a small club in his hand, saying, "Now hit that tree." It was a huge hickory. To the father's amazement the tree fell, and everything else the little boy struck was crushed or killed. The child was delighted and cried no more.

The next morning, before he went hunting, the father said, "Now, my boys, you must not go north. The Naked Bear lives in that direction. You must never go there." As soon as the father was out of sight, the little brother said, "Let's go north," and they started at once.

About midday the boys began to find huge paw prints, like a bear's but bigger. "It's the Naked Bear," said the older brother, "and its power is very great. Whenever anyone looks at its tracks, no matter how far off, it knows it and comes back to kill that person." As the little brother listened, he said, "I want to see it."

Soon he saw something enormous ahead of him. It had no hair on its body. Its skin was as smooth as a man's. When it came to a tree, it would jump at it, tearing it apart, and the pieces would fly in all directions. The smaller trees just fell at its touch.

It drew so near that the boy could feel its breath. He dodged from tree to tree, then darted off straight, running swiftly, with the bear close behind him, until he came to a stream that looked very deep.

He could just jump over it. So he sprang across, and the bear leaped after him. Then he sprang back to the other side, and the bear did the same. Again and again they crossed over, back and forth.

Now, as the boy jumped, he felt his strength increasing, while he saw that the bear was getting weaker. Knowing that it followed not by sight but by scent alone, he began running in a great loop on each side of the stream, and the bear followed in his track.

Worn out at last, it slipped as it landed on the bank, and as it scrambled to regain its balance, the boy saw the white spot on its forefoot, where it carried its heart.

Taking careful aim, he shot an arrow. The bear staggered and fell. Rising again, it struggled, then fell over dead.

After taking three hairs from its whiskers, the boys skinned it and smoked the hide thoroughly over a fire, so that it could not come back to life. In the evening, when they returned to the lodge, the younger brother handed his father the three whiskers, saying, "We have killed the Naked Bear, of which you were so much afraid."

The father was angry. "You must not go north again," he said, "and you must not go west. It is very dangerous there, too."

The next day, when the father had gone hunting again, the little boy said, "I'd like to see what there is in the west. Let's go."

After traveling westward all morning, the two brothers came to an extremely tall pine tree. In the top of this tree was a nest made of skins. "Oh," said the little brother, "what a strange place for a bed. Let me climb up and take a look." And up he went.

Two little Thunder children were lying in the nest, a male and a female. They were frightened. The boy pinched the male, and it cried out, "Father, father, a strange boy is scaring me to death."

Suddenly a voice was heard in the far west. It was Thunder. The moment it reached the nest, the boy struck it with his war club, and it fell dead to the ground. Then he pinched the little female, causing it to cry out, "Mother, mother!"

Instantly the mother Thunder's voice came out of the sky, and a moment later she stood at the nest. The boy clubbed her, and she, too, fell over dead. Then the boy said in his mind, "This male Thunder child will make a beautiful tobacco pouch for my father."

That evening, when the brothers returned, the little one said, "Father, here is your pouch."

"What?" cried the father when he saw the dead Thunder baby. "For this the Thunders will destroy us all."

"Oh, no," said the little boy. "They will not hurt us. I finished off that whole family."

The father took the skin for a pouch. Then he said, "Now, my sons, you must never go north to the country of the Stone Coats." So the next morning, when the father had left, the little one said, "Let's go."

But this time he went alone. His brother was too afraid.

After he had traveled awhile, he heard the loud barking of Stone Coat's dog. Quickly he jumped into a hollow log and lay still. "There's nothing here," said Stone Coat when he came along. But the dog kept barking.

Finally Stone Coat split the log with his club. "What a strange little creature you are," said Stone Coat, staring at the boy as he came out. "You are not big enough to fill a hole in my tooth."

"I did not come to fill holes in your teeth," said the boy, straining to look up at the enormous Stone Coat, who carried two bears in his belt the way an ordinary man would carry a couple of squirrels.

"Well," said Stone Coat, "let's see who can kick this log. If I can do it, and you can't, I'll eat you."

"If I can kick it higher than you, may I kill you?" asked the boy.

"Oh, yes."

"You try first," said the boy.

Putting his foot under the log, the Stone Coat kicked it twice his own height. Then the boy, placing his own foot under the log, sent it whistling through the air. It was gone a long time. When it came back down, it hit Stone Coat on the head and finished him off.

"Come here," said the little boy to Stone Coat's dog. This dog was as tall as a deer. But it came to him quickly, and the boy got on its back and rode it home, saying, "Now my father will have a good hunting dog."

When the father saw the dog, he cried, "What have you done? Stone Coat will kill us all."

"I have killed Stone Coat," said the boy.

"Very well," said the father, "but remember this: You must never go east. There's gambling there."

The next morning the older brother again refused to go. But the little one started out. Traveling east, he came to beautiful meadows, a great level country, where Wolf and Bear clans were playing ball on one side against Eagle, Turtle, and Beaver clans on the other.

The little boy took the side of the Wolf and Bear people. "If you win for us, you will own all this country," they said. They played, and he won for them.

Running home to the old lodge in the woods, he said to his father, "I have won all the beautiful country of the east. You come and be chief of it."

"Very well," said the father. Then he traveled to the east country with the two boys, and there they lived.

Now, that is the story.

Last Remaining

Sickness had killed many people, and the Being Without a Face had touched the father and mother of two children, who lived deep in the woods far from villages. The children, a boy named Last Remaining and his little sister, were left alone to take care of themselves.

One morning, when the little girl was swinging in a grapevine cradle, a song came floating over the hill. As the boy looked out the door, he saw an old woman climbing down the hill, singing as she came. He did not like the sounds in her song.

Still singing, she came up to the little girl and showed her a bowl of pudding, telling her to try it. The child held out her hands and was about to take the bowl when her brother rushed out and stopped her.

"The woman is a witch," he whispered to his sister. "If you eat her food, you will come under her power."

Furious, the witch backed away and began to shout. "Tomorrow I will come into the lodge and eat her before your eyes," she said. "Now, remember my promise!" They could hear her screaming as she disappeared through the trees.

The next morning the boy took an arrow out of his quiver and removed the head. Then he shook his sister until she was small, put her into the arrow, and replaced the head, saying, "The arrow will strike a stone at the end of the world. It will burst, and you will come out. Then run toward the south as fast as you can. I will overtake you."

Putting his arrow on the bowstring, he drew it and sent the arrow to the east. At that moment the call of a flicker was heard. The feathers on the arrow had been taken from that bird, and all the way the arrow sang with its voice.

Glancing up, the boy could see the arrow's trail. It looked like a rainbow in the sky. He took a long leap, and as he leaped, he ran into the air, far above the woods, following the trail. Looking back, he could see that the trail rolled up and dissolved in a mist as he ran along.

Now, when the witch came again and began looking for the little girl and could not find her, she became enraged. Running into the woods, she muttered, "The world is so small they cannot escape me. I will follow them everywhere." And with that she changed herself into a bear of enormous size and power.

Looking into the sky, she saw tracks. Although the trail of the arrow was lost, the boy's footprints remained on the clouds. In the form of a bear the old woman followed the tracks, keeping her eyes on the sky, until she came to the stone where the arrow had struck. Running on, she found the place where the boy and his sister had met.

The two were not far away, and as they stopped to rest, they heard a bear roar, and the roar said, "You can't get away from me. I'll find you wherever you are."

As he listened to these words, the boy opened his fawn-skin pouch and took out a pigeon feather. Throwing it behind him, he made this prayer: "Immediately let there be a roost of pigeons here, and let their numbers be so great that their droppings form a wall across

the world half as high as the tallest tree."

No sooner had he spoken than many thousands of wild pigeons came to roost, and the air was filled with their cries, gok, gok, gok, gok, and the sound of their wings, dum-m-m-m.

When the bear arrived at the roosting place, there before her was the ridge of droppings, half as high as the tallest tree. At first she tried to run around it, saying, "There has never been a time when a pigeon roost stretched across the world." But after running a long while, she became exhausted and returned to the place where the tracks of the boy and his sister disappeared beneath the ridge. Then she lay down to sleep.

In the morning the ridge had vanished. There was nothing to be seen but a single pigeon feather lying on the ground. The monster bit it and chewed it to pieces. Then she ran on, placing her paws in the boy's tracks, causing him to reel and stagger, for the body of the bear was filled with power.

Then the boy rubbed his sister's head, saying, "Let my sister become a cloud." At once she became a cloud and rested on his hand, while with the other hand he rubbed it off in the direction it was to go.

The bear was right behind him now and was just reaching out to him when the boy fell into a hole in the ground—or so it seemed to him. "Well, I am near my end," he thought.

But he kept falling, and as he fell, he grew sleepy. Looking up, he saw the monster coming down the side of the hole, winding round and round. Then the boy's eyes began to close, and he went to sleep, and as he slept, the Great Defender appeared to him.

"O grandfather," said the boy, "save me. The bear is after me." The Great Defender held out his hand for tobacco, and the boy gave him some. Then the spirit pointed toward a high cliff where smoke was coming out.

After a long time the boy woke up. He was falling, falling, and the monster was still behind him. At last he landed on his feet. He had come out of the hole, it seemed, and when he looked around, he saw a beautiful country. The bear was close behind.

Suddenly he saw a rock cliff in front of him, and in the cliff was an open cavern, where smoke was coming out. A woman was standing at the entrance, saying, "Be strong, my son. You will live if you come inside." It was the boy's own mother, and beside her stood a man.

"I am your father," said the man. "We were rescued from death by the Great Defender."

"And I am your sister," said a voice from the back of

the cavern. "Remember? You sent me off in the form of a cloud."

At that moment the bear came running up to the edge of the cavern and, crouching low, pushed its nose toward the fire. The mother quickly poured a ladleful of hot oil on the bear's face, and the pain made the monster fall over backward. Then she picked up the kettle and poured boiling oil until the bear lay still, and when the boy placed his foot on the bear's body, the whole carcass moved back and forth, showing that the animal was dead.

After that, the family returned to their old home, where they lived happily from then on. They were not bothered by witches.

The length of my story is now finished.

Porcupine's Grandson

In the ancient days, it is said, there lived a bad father and his stepson. The man did not love this boy and even hated to give him food. "You eat like a wolf," he would say. "I have to feed you all the time."

"Ah-kehhh," sighed the little boy, "someday I will be a hunter and will bring home meat when you are too old to find any. Will you want me then?"

The stepfather did not answer but merely kept on breathing. In his mind he was thinking how he would get rid of the boy. The next morning he said, "Would you like to go out with me today?" The son was pleased and said yes.

The two walked for some time through short trees and bushes. Deep woods were nowhere to be seen. Worried, the boy said, "I always thought hunters went to the deep woods, not the bushes."

"Stop worrying," said the stepfather, "I am an old hunter and know my business. Hurry up, walk faster, I will show you a wonderful place."

Suddenly the father stopped. He pretended to be excited and said, "Look, here's a hole. Hurry, crawl in and catch the game."

Thinking he would at last be a hunter, the boy dropped on his hands and knees and crawled forward. As soon as his heels were in, the stepfather closed up the hole with heavy stones. Then he turned around and walked home.

The boy was so frightened he began to cry. He pushed against the stones, but they were too big for him to move. Weak from crying and from having had nothing to eat that day, he was nearly fainting when he heard a voice in the dark saying, "Grandson, don't cry. We will try to do something for ourselves."

As he moved toward the voice, he heard "Don't come behind me, for my back is to be feared," and in this way he knew that the voice was a porcupine's.

Reaching into a bag that he had at his side, the old man porcupine pulled out something rolled up and handed it to the boy to eat. It was slippery-elm bark. The boy took it, ate some, and thought it was good. He ate until he was no longer hungry. "I don't know what your people like," said the old man, "but this is the kind of thing I usually like myself."

Then the porcupine said, "Grandson, I will go to the mouth of the hole and try to open it." But when he got to the place where the hole was stopped up, he found he could not push the stones. They were too heavy. "I will try another way," he said.

The stones were large, and there were openings between them. The porcupine stuck his nose between two of the stones and said charm words, calling all the animals to come help:

> toward here
>
> you are coming
>
> you brave ones

Soon there were noises outside the hole and a voice saying, "We want to know who will roll the stones away." Birds came and pecked at the stones, but they could do nothing. Small animals scratched, and nothing happened. A wolf said, "I am the man to do it," but his claws were not strong enough.

Finally a bear said, "It is my turn," and hugging the stones, she pulled them away. But when she looked in and saw a live boy, she jumped back, and all the animals began to run.

The old porcupine called to them, "Don't be afraid. This boy is poor. He has no mother." Slowly the animals returned.

"Who will take care of my grandson?" asked the old man. "Which of you has the same kind of food as his people? Which of you will be his mother?"

The turkey held out some seeds, but the boy remained silent. Next a female raccoon came up with a crawfish in her mouth. This seemed good to the boy, and he was about to take it, but the old porcupine said, "Wait. Keep waiting."

A female wolf heard the old man's voice and said to the boy, "My child, I have come for you. I will take care of you because my food is meat."

"No," said the porcupine, "you would just eat the child." Then the bear said, "I will take care of him myself," and it seemed to the boy that the bear took him by the hand and that she was just like a person. She had two cubs who followed along beside her, and the four of them went off together.

That night the boy slept between the bear and her two cubs. When the boy was hungry, the bear gave him a honeycomb and some blackberry flatcakes. When he was thirsty, she gave him her paw to suck.

During the day, while the mother lay sleeping in the sun and the three brothers were at play, the cubs would pull the boy's nails to make them long like theirs. That way they could all run up trees together.

One time the mother awoke and couldn't see the boy. Looking everywhere, she found him high in a tree a long way off. Then she scolded her cubs and pushed the boy's nails back to their original size.

When blackberries were ripe, the mother picked as many as she could and spread them out to dry in the sun. Then she pressed them into flatcakes as big around as a bear's paw. "We can live now, for we have plenty of food," she said. And so the many days of summer passed.

Winter came, and the mother found a hollow tree with

an opening at the top. When they had all climbed up and settled down inside, the boy looked around and thought the place seemed roomy and comfortable.

Here they remained, and the boy and the cubs played together and were happy. The mother slept most of the time. But once when she heard a sound, she woke instantly and said, "You must keep very still. There is a hunter near."

In the tree was an opening where the mother could look out. Shading her eyes with her paw, she kept watch. When she heard dry leaves rattle and saw the hunter approach, she said to the boy, "Now I am about to tell you something. Look at what belongs to me. Examine it carefully." Putting her paw into her pocket, she took out a stick with two prongs. "This is how we use it," she said.

Then she held the two prongs toward herself and pointed the straight part toward the hunter. "If he comes in a line toward the end of the stick," she said, "he is forced outward in the direction of one prong or the other. That way he passes around our hiding place without seeing us."

The bear kept moving the stick back and forth until the hunter had gone.

All went well until one day the bear said, "Our time

has come. We must soon leave each other." A hunter was moving in a straight path toward the tree, and although the mother held out her forked stick, the hunter was not turned aside.

"It is your stepfather," she said, "your own stepfather." She moved the stick back and forth, but it could do no good. Her power was gone. The stick itself broke apart, and there was now nothing in the way.

Turning to the boy, the mother said, "You can stay here, but we must go, for we are bears." Then she said to the older cub, "You go first, your brother will follow."

The boy saw everything clearly. The little bear climbed out of the tree. The boy heard the snap of the bowstring and the sound of the arrow as it hit, and as he watched the bear, it seemed to throw off a burden. Then it dropped to the ground, while the bear itself went straight on without stopping.

The other cub followed. Again the boy heard the arrow and saw the bear's body fall. But the bear itself ran on.

Then the mother said to the boy, "I must leave you now. May you have good dreams." She rushed out and began running toward the west. Just as before, the boy heard the bowstring and the sound of the arrow as it pierced her heart. The bear straightened out and died, but her own self sped forward like the wind on its journey.

After a moment, the boy climbed down the tree. "Father," he asked, "are you going to shoot me, too?"

Seeing his stepson, the man was frightened. He said, "Why didn't you come out first? Why didn't you tell me the bears were your relatives?" Then he cried, "Ah-kehhh, now I will always have bad luck."

The man knew that the boy had power, and he asked him to come home with him to protect him from the bear ghosts. "Do you want me now?" asked the boy.

"Yes," said the man, "I need you."

He never dared hunt again. But the boy did.

That is all.

The Quilt of Men's Eyes

In ancient times there was a family of seven brothers and one sister living contentedly in a large bark lodge. While the brothers were out hunting, the sister would cut firewood in the forest nearby. Usually this sister would be the first to return in the evening. The brothers, who had to go far to find game, did not come home until very late.

Now, the youngest of the brothers was one who was hidden in the husks, so it is said. And being kept as a magic child, always out of sight, he never left the lodge.

One day a young woman, the daughter of a known witch, arrived carrying a basket of marriage bread. Of course, the lodge was empty except for the one who was hidden in the husks.

The witch's daughter had been instructed by her mother to take her seat on the bed of this youngest brother, which was closest to the doorway. But instead, she chose the third bed down, imagining that it had a better appearance.

After a few moments she moved to a different bed, thinking it looked a little finer, and she kept on shifting her position until she finally came to the seventh bed. Here the brothers and their sister found her when they returned to the lodge that night.

Seeing the basket of marriage bread, they all addressed her as sister-in-law, except for the oldest brother, on whose bed she was sitting. He called her wife.

At once the young woman noticed that the man she had chosen was blind in one eye. Then she was angry at herself for not having obeyed her mother's instructions. But it was too late now to change her mind.

Looking around, she saw that someone she had not noticed before was lying on the bed next to the doorway, the very bed on which she had been told to sit. She also discovered that this young man was the one who was noble in the family, that in fact he was hidden in the husks, meaning he was secluded from all persons. His body was completely covered in skin robes from head to foot, and nobody paid him the slightest attention.

The next day, when the others were out of the lodge, the bride wife got up from her bed and went over to the place where the covered figure was lying. Cautiously she drew down the covering, and there, with desiring eyes, she saw a handsome, finely developed young man, fast asleep.

For a long while she stood there, bending over him, desiring him very much. Then she shook him gently and said, "Get up, friend. Let us talk."

But the young man would neither get up nor speak to her, no matter how hard she begged. Naturally, this only increased her desire.

That evening, when the family had returned for the night and had eaten their supper of corn bread, deer meat, and spicebush tea, the bride began to tell her husband a story she had invented. She declared that the one who was hidden in the husks had come over to her side of the fire and had spoken to her in an improper manner and that she had had to summon all her strength to push him away. As she spoke, her husband listened quietly.

The next day the woman again coaxed the young man, and this time he woke up and talked to her, telling her she should be satisfied with the one she had chosen as her husband. Enraged, she went back to her side of the lodge and bruised and scratched her face with her own hands.

When her husband came home, she told him that this time the hidden one had attacked her. Again the husband listened quietly, but he already knew what he would have to do.

The following day he told the others what he had heard from his wife and how her face had been scratched and bruised, and they all agreed that their youngest brother would have to be killed. As soon as they got back to the lodge, they informed him of their decision, and although he knew he was innocent, he calmly lay down so that they could take his life.

Then the oldest drew his flint knife across the youngest brother's throat. He pressed firmly, but it made no cut. He tried again and sawed away until the knife was worn out. Then the next brother tried, and he, too, failed, and when all the brothers had tried and failed, the youngest began to speak.

"None of you can succeed in this," he said. "My sister alone has the power. Let her try, and when she has killed me, you must build a massive lodge, putting over it a roof of the largest logs so that it will be entirely secure. But before making the roof, you must lay my body inside and also leave my sister with me." Then the sister took her flint knife and cut off her brother's head, immediately stepping back in great sorrow.

When the log house had been prepared, the six brothers went back to their lodge, only to find that the bride of the oldest brother had mysteriously disappeared. While they were wondering where she had gone, there arose a terrific windstorm, caused by the witch who was the mother of the missing bride. The storm snapped branches and ripped off the leaves of trees.

Inside the house of great logs the dead brother's head suddenly joined his body, and the young man came alive. Then he said to his sister, "O sister, press your hands over my face."

The sister pressed as hard as she could, knowing that the storm maidens would try to snatch away her brother's eyes. The storm swept the ground in all directions, uprooting trees and tossing them like blades of grass. The lodge of the six brothers was torn to pieces, and all six were destroyed with it.

When the storm had passed, the young man said to his sister, "You may as well take your hands from my face. It was no use for you to have held them there. The witch has beaten me. Her magic was greater than mine." Astonished, the sister lifted her hands and saw that her brother's eyes were gone.

The brother and sister now traveled southward, camping each night for three days. When the sister found wild turkeys, she would hand her blind brother his bow and arrows and turn his body in the right direction, and he would shoot them. Then she would dress the turkeys and cook them over a fire. On the fourth day the sister saw in the distance a moss-covered lodge.

"Brother, I see a lodge," she said. "Next to it stands a tall chestnut tree, and there is a lake on the other side. Shall we go that way?"

"Yes," he said. "It is the lodge where we lived when we were children."

Inside they found all the things that were common to the lodges of those ancient times: clay pots, baskets, wooden mortars, tubs of corn and beans, and bundles of spicebush twigs for making tea.

On the evening of the third day after they had reached their old home, a handsome young man arrived and made a proposal of marriage to the sister. The visitor did not appear ill at ease but stood in the lodge wherever it seemed good to him. With her brother's consent the young woman accepted the stranger's proposal, and in due course she gave birth to twin boys.

Now, the moment the children were born, their mother threw them into the lake. As they touched the water they began to paddle and quickly swam to shore. Again she threw them into the water, and in a moment they were back again. Then she threw them far out into the lake. When they swam to shore, she said, "That will do."

They now began to run around and play, and after a while their uncle said to them, "I wish I could see the two of you. But as you can tell, I have no eyes."

"Oh, uncle!" said the twins. "We will try to make you see us." Then each of the boys took out one of his own eyes and placed it in his uncle's head. "I see you both!" he cried, and when he had handed the eyes back to them, they answered, "Now we will go get you your own. Where are they?"

"They are in cloudland," said the uncle, "where a witch and her daughters are making a quilt of men's eyes. Remember this: the two that are mine are partly blood-shot."

Then the twins collected a great quantity of swamp grass and piled it up, and when they had enough, they set it on fire, jumped into the flames, and were carried upward on huge clouds of smoke. Rising higher and higher, they were soon in cloudland, where they came down in the form of cinders.

Changing themselves into fleas, they crept into the witch's lodge, and there, to one side, they saw the quilt of eyes, all alive and winking. On the other side of the fire the witch and her daughters were pounding corn with wooden corn pounders.

Still in the form of fleas, the boys crawled up the women's legs and began to bite them. "You're pinching me," said the mother to one of her daughters, and in a

moment they were all making accusations, shouting and hitting each other with the pounders.

When the witches had completely destroyed themselves, the twins went over to the quilt and easily picked out their uncle's eyes. Then they ran to the place where they had to descend, and again becoming fleas, they used the seed heads of dandelions as parachutes and floated back to earth.

Going directly to their uncle, they returned his eyes

to him, and the uncle and the boys looked at each other and were glad. After that the uncle and his sister and her husband and the twin boys all lived together in the moss-covered lodge. The men hunted and brought home much meat, fine furs, and feather robes.

Now I finish my tale. So it is enough. Now, moreover, we will lie down to sleep.

Turtle and His Sister

What?

All right, here is another.

In a lodge well stocked with oil, deer, and bear meat three winds were living with their older brother, Great Wind. Not far away lived Turtle and his sister.

One morning the youngest of the winds said to his brothers, "I am going over to Turtle's lodge." The brothers, knowing he had marriage plans, replied, "It is well."

So he got himself ready, took a pouch filled with bear oil, slung it over his shoulder, and started off. Turtle's sister was at home when he arrived at her lodge.

"I want to marry you," he said, sitting down beside her. She gave no answer and acted as though she did not see him. While he sat waiting for her reply, he kept dipping his finger into the pouch and licking off the oil.

He remained all day at her side, sucking his finger as he waited patiently. When night came, she answered, "I have decided not to marry you." Returning to his brothers, he told them what her reply had been.

Then the next youngest brother said, "It must be I of whom she is thinking," and in the morning, taking a pouch filled with oil, he went over to the neighboring lodge. Finding the young woman at home, he sat down next to her, saying, "I have come to marry you. Will you be my wife?"

No answer. Patiently he waited through the entire day, dipping his fingers from time to time. When it was nearly dark, she gave him the same answer she had given his brother, and he went home.

That night the third brother said, "It must be I of whom she is thinking. I shall go there tomorrow." And he did. But in the evening, just like the others, he returned without success.

Then Turtle said to his sister, "You have made a terrible mistake. The next one who comes will be Great Wind himself. You should have accepted his youngest brother. Now it is too late."

In the morning Great Wind said to his brothers, "Obviously it is I of whom she is thinking," and he started off toward Turtle's lodge. Finding the sister at home, he said, "My wife, I have come for you. You must go home with me now."

Bitterly she resisted him as he seized her arm and tried to pull her along. Turtle, her brother, was at one end of the fire, hiding under the ashes. While Great Wind was struggling with her, the young woman managed to steer him toward the fire so that he stepped on Turtle, who immediately bit his toe.

"Brother-in-law, let go of my toe," he said. But Turtle hung on to it. Picking up a log, he beat Turtle on the head, and in that moment Turtle grew bigger and bit more of the toe. As he beat him again, he grew bigger still and bit the whole foot.

Not realizing what was happening, Great Wind kept pounding away until Turtle, growing bigger and bigger, had swallowed his entire body. Then Turtle rested, and two days later Great Wind passed through and came out the other end.

"After ten days he will regain consciousness and start chasing us," said Turtle, "so we had better leave now." The sister, putting Turtle into a basket and strapping it to her back, started off as fast as she could go.

Ten days later, when Great Wind woke up, he began to follow the young woman's tracks. Hearing him in the distance, Turtle said to his sister, "He's coming fast. Leave me here, and keep going."

Soon Great Wind came along and stepped on Turtle without seeing him. Turtle bit him again.

"Brother-in-law! Let go of my foot," he cried, and he kicked him against a fallen tree. But with every kick Turtle got bigger and bit more, until at last Great Wind was swallowed again, and once again he passed through after two days.

Now, as the sister was walking along, far ahead, she was surprised to see Turtle sitting in her path. He had gotten there before her by means of his magic power.

Together they went on, and when another ten days were up, Great Wind regained consciousness and continued the chase.

Once again Turtle swallowed him, waited for him to pass through, then rejoined his sister, climbing back into her basket. By this time, however, the sister was growing faint and exhausted. When she saw light ahead and realized she had come to a lake, she said to herself, "If I have to die, I may as well die here," and with these words she sat down on a stone.

Soon after that, Great Wind came up behind her and exclaimed, "My wife, you are waiting for me!" Overjoyed, he took some tobacco from his pouch and burned it as an offering to the stone on which the poor sister was sitting.

Praying to it, he spoke the words, "I thank you, because you made my wife wait for me here." He kept on thanking the stone as he went back toward the woods, burning tobacco to the other stones as well.

Just then a strange man rose out of the lake and called to the young woman, "Quick! Come with me!" Without hesitation she followed him into the water, and when Great Wind turned toward the lake again, she was gone. Nothing remained but her tracks leading to the water's edge.

At the bottom of the lake stood a lodge where the strange man lived with his sister. Following the man inside, the young woman hung up her basket and sat down next to it. When she was given food, she dropped a few pieces into the basket for Turtle.

Noticing this, the man's sister asked, "Why do you put food there?"

"My brother is in the basket," she replied. Then came the question, "Can I see him?"

"Wait two days" was the answer. "Then he will come out as a fully formed man."

Just as predicted, Turtle became a man and stepped out of the basket in two days. Afterward he lived with the strange man's sister as her husband, and his own sister became the wife of the man in the lake himself, the one who had rescued her from Great Wind.

This is the end of the story of Turtle and his sister.

Notes

The abbreviation C&H stands for Curtin and Hewitt, "Seneca Fiction." This and other works referred to by author and title or by author only will be found fully listed in the References.

Introduction

Page x/storytelling customs: Parker, *Seneca Myths,* pp. xxvi, 98–99. Page x/"tie off the bag": William N. Fenton, personal communication, 1985. Page xii/Morgan on Iroquois political influence: Morgan, p. 3. Page xii/"Indian of Indians" . . . "classics": Parker in Converse, pp. 9–10. Page xiii/George Washington on Iroquois dance: Myers, pp. 62–63. Page xv/on the origin of Stone Coats: Parker, *Seneca Myths,* p. 394; cf. Converse, p. 74. Page xvi/story of a strange boy: C&H, p. 345. Page xviii/"There's a problem . . .": Hubert Buck, Sr., personal communication, 1985. Page xviii/*onehsa* defined as "fungus": Chafe, no. 1147 (p. 69).

Stories

Page 3/Chestnut Pudding, from C&H, nos. 24 and 109; Fenton, p. 109; and Parker, *Seneca Myths,* no. 14; with details from C&H, nos. 41 (p. 199) and 117 (p. 583).

The first half of the story resembles the European folktale known as The Magic Mill (Aarne and Thompson, no. 565). At least a dozen Iroquoian variants have been recorded, including one from the descendants of the Huron, now in Oklahoma, suggesting that French settlers may have brought the tale to Canada two or even three centuries ago.

Page 11/Two Feathers, from C&H, nos. 20, 22, 50, 109, and 137; and Parker, *Seneca Myths,* no. 21.

Known to folklorists as Dirty Boy (Thompson, no. 48), the tale of a young hero whose intended bride is taken by an impostor was told by most of the northern Plains tribes, including the Cheyenne, the Sioux, and the Blackfeet. The shaman uncle and the hero's elaborate garments are distinctive features of the Iroquois variants.

Page 19/The Whirlwinds and the Stone Coats, from C&H, no. 67; and Parker, *Seneca Myths,* no. 55; with details from C&H, nos. 131 and 132.

This is a good example of the double story, a form widely used by Indian storytellers. In this case the narrator tells how a Stone Coat's visit to the Whirlwinds' lodge leads to trouble, but in the end the Whirlwinds are the winners. Then the plot begins all over again with the visit of another Stone Coat, leading to more trouble and another victory for the Whirlwinds. For more on double stories, see Bierhorst, *The Red Swan,* p. 10.

Page 24/Animal-Foot Hitter, from C&H, nos. 57, 109, and 111; and Parker, *Seneca Myths,* nos. 20 and 21; with details from C&H, nos. 41 (p. 215) and 118 (p. 607).

In the distant past this tale may have traveled from the Chippewa to the Seneca, who reshaped it while keeping the basic elements: youngest brother forbidden to hunt, magic arrows, arrows shot away in vain attempt to kill bird, bird controlled by sorcerer, sorcerer offers young woman as bride, hero brings young woman home. The Chippewa tale, known as The Red Swan, is reprinted in Bierhorst, *The Red Swan,* pp. 277–94. Variants, mostly from Midwest tribes, are listed in Bierhorst, *The Mythology of North America,* p. 252.

Page 31/Turtle's War Party, from C&H, no. 6; and Parker, *Seneca Myths,* no. 40; with details from C&H, nos. 47 (p. 241) and 132 (p. 658).

According to the Iroquois story of Creation, mud that was laid on the turtle's back expanded until it became the present earth. But in Iroquois folktales Turtle is a trickster. The story of Turtle's war party (Thompson, no. 38) was told by tribes throughout the Plains and the

Great Lakes region. (In Turtle's war song the words "black face," referring to Rattlesnake, may contain a double meaning: Black Face is a name for any rattlesnake; also, homecoming warriors blackened their faces as a sign of victory.)

Page 37 / The Mother of Ghosts, from C&H, no. 116; with details from nos. 73 (p. 406) and 132 (p. 691).

Stories in which an attempt is made to bring a loved one back from the dead land are found throughout North America (Thompson, no. 55; Fisher, no. VII-1). This Seneca version is unusual on two counts; the attempt is successful and the loved one, typically the wife, is here the husband.

Page 44 / Cannibal Island, from C&H, nos. 28, 41, 71, and 135; Curtin, pp. 134–45; and Smith, pp. 64–69; with details from C&H, nos. 58 (p. 312), 90 (p. 451), and 109 (p. 518), and from Parker, *Seneca Myths,* nos. 13 (p. 125) and 33 (p. 277).

Most Iroquois storytellers have been men. But a very full version of this popular Seneca tale was told by Mrs. Phoebe Logan, about 1880 (Smith, pp. 64–69). It was Mrs. Logan's husband, Sim, who gave Seneca lessons to Jeremiah Curtin in 1883.

Page 52 / The Moose Wife, from C&H, no. 64 (pp. 361–65); with details from nos. 5 (p. 91) and 135 (pp. 751–52), from Curtin, p. 395, and from Parker, *Seneca Myths,* no. 70 (p. 395).

Stories of hunters who are unfaithful to their animal wives are found throughout central and northeastern North America. Buffalo Wife is typical of the Plains (Thompson, no. 57), while Deer Wife has been reported from New England and the western Great Lakes (Fisher, no. IX-9).

Page 60 / The Boy Who Learned the Songs of Birds, from C&H, nos. 42 (pp. 226–27), 55, 73 (pp. 408–9), and 137 (p. 755); and Curtin, p. 179; with details from C&H, nos. 26 (p. 158), 38 (p. 193), and 42 (p. 224).

The manner in which the little brother wears his two turkey feathers suggests the traditional headgear for the Great Feather Dance, one of the Four Sacred Rituals of the Iroquois, still being performed in New

York and on the Six Nations Reserve. Today, however, dancers may wear Plains-style headdresses imported from Oklahoma.

Page 67 / Turtle Goes Hunting, from Curtin, pp. 293–96.

Notice that Turtle escapes by using the same trick as in Turtle's War Party. The mistake of trying to drown a turtle recurs in folktales throughout North America and eastern Asia (Thompson, pp. 302–3).

Page 72 / Mother Swan's Daughters, from C&H, nos. 29 and 39; with details from nos. 99 (p. 463) and 137 (pp. 751–52).

In his classic study of the Iroquois, Lewis Morgan explains that marriages were agreed upon by the mothers. Fathers had nothing to do with the arrangements, and even the bride and groom were not consulted. In many cases young brides were given to old men, a custom which became increasingly unpopular and which is perhaps reflected in the comical episode of the older man who tries to marry Mother Swan's daughters. The custom of taking two brides at once, often encountered in folktales, was strictly forbidden, according to Morgan (p. 324).

Page 79 / Lodge Boy and Thrown Away, from C&H, no. 34; the Naked Bear episode has been drawn from nos. 8 (p. 98), 48 (p. 259), and 59 (pp. 342–43).

Lodge Boy and Thrown Away (Thompson, no 44) is the name used by folklorists to designate an important tale told by Plains Indians, some of whom elevated it to the status of a myth. Scattered variants have been reported from the tribes of British Columbia and the eastern woodlands, including the Chippewa and the Cherokee, as well as the Iroquois.

Page 87 / Last Remaining, from Parker, *Seneca Myths,* no. 57; and C&H, nos. 57 and 129; with details from Curtin, pp. 309 and 443–48, and from C&H, no. 103 (pp. 478 and 480).

The so-called magic flight, in which a hero drops objects that become obstacles to his pursuer, is a worldwide motif (Thompson, pp. 333–34). But the dropped feather that becomes a pigeon roost is typically Iroquoian. The pigeon-dung ridge as an impassable obstacle, though fantastic, gains a measure of credibility if it is recalled that passenger pigeons were once so numerous that a single flock could darken the sky. Overhunted, the birds for all practical purposes were extinct by the 1890s.

Page 93 / Porcupine's Grandson, from Parker, *Seneca Myths,* no. 18; C&H, no. 66; and Barbeau, nos. 35–37; with details from Smith, p. 44, and from C&H, no. 127 (pp. 658–59).

The story of the cruelly abandoned boy helped by a porcupine and mothered by a bear is one of the most popular of all Iroquoian tales, with variants reported from Cayuga (Waugh, no. 48), Onondaga, Seneca, and Huron sources.

Page 101 / The Quilt of Men's Eyes, from C&H, nos. 102 and 114; with details from Parker, *Seneca Myths,* no. 10, and from Beauchamp, p. 204.

The custom of secluding a child in order to increase its spiritual power is well known in Iroquois myth and folklore. In Seneca stories such a child is called "down-fended." In Onondaga lore the term is "hidden in the husks." There is no evidence that the custom was ever carried out in real life. Distinctively Iroquois, this story nevertheless incorporates standard elements, including the widespread motif known as Potiphar's wife (Thompson, pp. 326–27), in which a woman makes vain overtures to a man and then accuses him of assaulting her.

Page 110 / Turtle and His Sister, from C&H, no. 63.

Great Wind, also called Great Defender, has the power to banish disease and is regularly prayed to in Seneca rituals. Yet in this unusual folktale he is portrayed as a buffoon.

A. Folktale Sources

Barbeau, Charles Marius. *Huron and Wyandot Mythology*. Canada, Department of Mines, Geological Survey, Memoir 80; Anthropological Series 11. 1915.

Beauchamp, William M. *Iroquois Folk Lore*. 1922. Reprint. Port Washington, N.Y.: Kennikat Press, 1965.

Converse, Harriet Maxwell. *Myths and Legends of the New York State Iroquois*. Edited by Arthur Caswell Parker. 1908. Reprint. Albany: New York State Museum, 1981.

Cornplanter, Jesse J. *Legends of the Longhouse*. 1938. Reprint. Port Washington, N.Y.: Ira J. Friedman, 1963.

Curtin, Jeremiah. *Seneca Indian Myths*. New York: E. P. Dutton, 1923.
    Eighty-nine stories, sixty-seven of which appear, revised, in Curtin and Hewitt (see below).

Curtin, Jeremiah, and J. N. B. Hewitt. "Seneca Fiction," edited by Hewitt, *32nd Annual Report of the Bureau of American Ethnology, 1910–1911*, pp. 37–819. 1918.

Fenton, William N. "Letters to an Ethnologist's Children," *New York Folklore Quarterly*, 4 (1948): 109–20.
    Four tales from the Six Nations Reserve.

Michelson, Karin, and Georgina Nicholas. *Three Stories in Oneida*. Canadian Ethnology Service, paper no. 73. 1981.

Parker, Arthur Caswell. *Rumbling Wings, and Other Indian Tales*. Garden City, N.Y.: Doubleday, 1928.
    This and Parker's *Skunny Wundy* (see page 122), both written for children, contain stories not published elsewhere.

————. *Seneca Myths and Folk Tales.* 1923. Reprint. New York: AMS Press, 1978.

————. *Skundy Wundy: Seneca Indian Tales.* 1927. Reprint. Chicago: Albert Whitman, 1970.

Smith, Erminnie A. *Myths of the Iroquois.* 1883. Reprint. Ohsweken, Ontario: Iroqrafts, 1983.

Waugh, F. W. Collection of Iroquois folklore. Manuscript 1666, American Philosophical Society, Philadelphia. 1912–1918.

> One hundred fifty-seven tales, almost all from the Six Nations Reserve. The manuscript is fully described in Martha C. Randle's "The Waugh Collection of Iroquois Folktales," *Proceedings of the American Philosophical Society,* 97 (1953): 611–33.

Williams, Marianne [Mithun], ed. *Kanien'kéha' Okara'shón: 'a* (Mohawk Stories). New York State Museum Bulletin 427. 1976.

B. Other Works

Aarne, Antti, and Stith Thompson. *The Types of the Folktale.* Helsinki: Academia Scientiarum Fennica, 1961.

Bierhorst, John. *The Mythology of North America.* New York: William Morrow, 1985.

————. *The Red Swan: Myths and Tales of the American Indians.* New York: Farrar, Straus and Giroux, 1976.

Catalog to Manuscripts at the National Anthropological Archives. Smithsonian Institution. 4 vols. Boston: G. K. Hall, 1975.

> Includes brief descriptions of the Iroquois manuscripts of Curtin, Hewitt, and others.

Chafe, Wallace L. *Seneca Morphology and Dictionary.* Washington: Smithsonian Press, 1967.

Fisher, Margaret W. "The Mythology of the Northern and Northeastern Algonkians." In Frederick Johnson, ed., *Man in Northeastern North*

America, Papers of the Robert S. Peabody Foundation for Archaeology 3: 226–62. Andover, Mass.: Phillips Academy, 1946.

Morgan, Lewis Henry. *League of the Iroquois.* 1851. Reprint. New York: Corinth, 1962.

Myers, Albert Cook, ed. *The Boy George Washington, Aged 16, His Own Account of an Iroquois Indian Dance, 1748.* Philadelphia: Albert Cook Myers, 1932.

Thompson, Stith. *Tales of the North American Indians.* 1929. Reprint. Bloomington: Indiana University Press, 1966.

Trigger, Bruce G., ed. *Handbook of North American Indians,* vol. 15: Northeast. Washington: Smithsonian Institution, 1978.

    Includes 250 pages on the Iroquois.

Weinman, Paul L. *A Bibliography of the Iroquoian Literature.* New York State Museum and Science Service, Bulletin 411. 1969.

    Includes more than a hundred titles on mythology and folklore.